Flight of Exiles

Other books by Ben Bova

Ben Bova

Flight of Exiles

E. P. Dutton & Co., Inc.   New York

Published simultaneously in Canada by Clarke,
Irwin & Company Limited, Toronto and Vancouver

SBN: 0-525-29865-7   LCC: 72-78092

Designed by Dorothea von Elbe
Printed in the U.S.A.
First Edition

To the Pratt family,
with thanks for fine times.

Chapter 1

"Fire . . . it's on *fire!*"

"EMERGENCY. EMERGENCY. EMERGENCY."

"Attention everyone. Emergency in cryonics area six. Damage Control and Life Support groups to cryonics area six immediately. Emergency."

"The whole area's a mass of flames! The standby equipment is out! Get more men up here, quick!"

The starship had no name. The people aboard merely called it "the ship." It had originally been a huge artificial satellite orbiting around Earth, a minor city in space, hugging close to the Mother World. Then it was made into a prison for thousands of the world's best scientists and their families. Now it was a starship, coasting silently from the solar system toward the triple star system, Alpha Centauri.

Inside the main control center, things were anything but quiet.

"There are fifty men and women in cryosleepers in number six area. If you can't get that fire under control they'll die."

Larry Belsen was standing up on the ship's bridge. It was actually a long curving row of desk consoles, where seated technicians worked the controls that watched and directed every section of the mammoth ship. Larry's job was as close to a ship's captain as any job on the ship; he was in charge of this Command and Control center, he had a finger on every pulsebeat in the ship.

The technicians were hunched over the keyboards, fingers flying over the buttons that electronically linked all of the great ship's machinery and people. In front of each of their desks were viewscreens that showed them pictures, graphs, charts, every kind of information from each compartment and piece of equipment aboard: engines, computers, life support, living quarters, work areas, cryonics units, power systems . . . all on view in the hundreds of screens.

Normally, Larry thought of the curving ring of screens as the eye of a giant electronic insect, multifaceted to see into all the areas of the ship. He had studied about Earth's insects briefly in a biology course, on the learning tapes. But now his attention was riveted to one particular screen, where the fire was raging in cryonics area six. There wasn't much he could see: smoke obscured almost everything.

He put a hand on the shoulder of the girl working that console.

"Can't you get the emergency equipment functioning?"

She was a thin, dark-skinned girl, with close-cropped hair. Glancing up at Larry, "It should've gone on automatically. But it won't respond at all. I've tried. . . ." Her eyes were wide with fear, anxiety.

"It's not your fault," Larry said calmly. "Don't blame yourself."

"But there are fifty sleepers in there!"

Larry shook his head. Without bothering to go across to the life support displays, he said, "They must be dead by now, Tania. No sense tearing yourself up over it."

He took a step to the guy sitting at the next desk console. "You in touch with the Damage Control group?"

"Yes . . . they've plugged into a wall phone out in the main corridor, just outside area six."

"Who's in charge?"

"It's Mort Campbell's unit, but he's not the one on the phone."

"Let me talk . . ."

"Is it cryonics six?"

Larry turned to see Dan Christopher at the door down at the far end of the bridge. For an instant, everything seemed to stand still: people frozen at the console desks, communications speakers quiet, viewscreens stilled.

The two of them looked almost like brothers, at first glance. Larry was tall and slim with dark hair that he kept clipped fairly short. His eyes, though, were a cold gray, like a granite rock floating in space far from the warmth of a star. Dan was the same height and also youthfully slim. His hair was a lighter shade, and almost shoulder length. It curled slightly. His eyes were fiercely black, deep and flashing. Both of them were wearing workshift coveralls: Larry's the blue-gray shade of the ship's Command and Control personnel, Dan's the howling orange of the Propulsion and Power section.

"Is it six?" Dan demanded, his voice rising.

Larry didn't answer; he merely nodded slowly.

"My father's in there!"

By now Larry had crossed the plastic tiled floor of the

bridge and was within arm's reach of Dan. He took him by the arm.

"So is mine! There's nothing you can do, Dan. The Damage Control group's already there, but . . ."

"My father!"

Dan pulled loose and yanked the door open. Larry stood there and watched him disappear down the corridor, running, until the door automatically slid shut again.

With a sad shake of his head, Larry went back to the control desks and viewscreens.

"You still in contact with the Damage Control party?"

The fellow nodded and pointed to the main screen over his desk, in the center of a group of seven screens. A scared-looking teenager was in view. He was looking somewhere off camera, coughing in the smoke that was drifting past him.

"What's going on up there?" Larry asked sharply.

The kid in the screen seemed to jerk with surprise. Then, turning full face toward the screen, he said:

"Mr. Campbell and the crew are in there. . . . I saw flames coming through the main hatch a few minutes ago, but there's only smoke now."

"Is anybody hurt?"

"I don't know. They're all inside there . . . nobody's come out."

"Did they have smoke masks?"

"Yeah . . ."

"Where's yours?" Larry asked.

The kid looked startled again. "I . . . uh . . . yeah, it's right here. . . . I got it. . . ."

More gently, Larry said, "Don't you think it might be a

good idea to put it on? It can't protect you while it's zipped to your belt."

Larry found that he was bending over the shoulder of the seated technician. He straightened up and glanced at the life support screens on the next console. They were blank, dead.

Fifty people in there. Dan's father . . . and my own.

"Larry . . . look."

He turned his attention back to the viewscreen. The Damage Control group was trudging wearily back into the corridor. Their faces were smudged, their coveralls blackened. The foamers and other fire-fighting equipment they dragged seemed to weigh tons.

There was hardly any smoke coming from the hatch now. The last man to step out into the corridor slowly unclipped his smoke mask. Larry recognized him as Mort Campbell: stocky, slow-moving but always sure of himself, one of the oldest men working on this shift—nearly thirty.

Then Dan Christopher came dashing into view. He pushed wordlessly past the first few men of the Damage Control group, his eyes wild, his mouth open in silent frenzy.

Campbell stopped him at the hatch. Dan tried to dodge around him, but Campbell grabbed Dan by his slim shoulders and held him firmly.

"Don't go in there. It's not pretty."

"My father . . ."

"They're all dead."

Watching them in the viewscreen, Larry felt his insides sink. *You knew he was dead,* he told himself. But knowing it in your head and feeling it in your guts are two entirely different things.

He knew all the technicians, all up and down the long row of consoles, were staring at him now. He stood unmoved, his face frozen into a mask of concentration, and kept his eyes on the viewscreen. Inside his head, he was telling himself over and over, *You never knew him. He was frozen before you were old enough to remember him. There's no reason for you to break up.*

Dan's reaction was very different.

"NO!" he screamed, and he twisted out of Campbell's grasp and darted into the still smoky cryonics area. The older man slipped his face mask back on and went in after him.

"The cameras inside the cryonics area aren't working now," the girl tech said quietly, her fingers still tapping on her keyboard, trying to coax life back into the dead machines.

"Never mind," Larry said woodenly. "There's nothing in there that we should see."

Chapter 2

Larry sat in his living quarters, in the dark. It was a single compartment, barely big enough for a bunk, a desk, and a chair. The bunk and desk were molded into the curving walls of the compartment. Drawers and sliding partitions to the closet and sanitary blended almost invisibly with the silvery metal of the walls.

In the darkness, as he sat in the only chair and stared at nothing, there was only the residual glow of the viewscreen at the foot of the bed and the faint fluorescence of the wall painting that Valery had done for him years ago, when he had first been assigned a compartment of his own.

So you've lost a father you've never known, Larry still argued with himself. *You're not the only one. Every one of those fifty frozen people was a father or mother to somebody aboard the ship. Look at Dan; it's hit him a lot harder.*

But as he thought about it, slowly Larry began to realize that something else was bothering him. It wasn't the deaths. Not really. That left nothing but a cold emptiness inside him. It was something else. . . .

What caused the fire?

According to the ship's computer records, they had

been crawling through the huge gulf of space for nearly fifty years. Twenty-some thousand human beings, exiles from Earth, on their way to Alpha Centauri in a giant pinwheel of a ship. Nearly fifty years. Almost there.

But the ship was starting to die.

The men and women who had started on this long, long voyage were exiles. They had been scientists— molecular geneticists, most of them. The world government had rounded them up and placed them in a prison, this ship, which was then only a mammoth satellite orbiting Earth. Earth was overcrowded, it needed peace and above all it needed stability. The scientists represented the forces of change, not stability. The geneticists and their colleagues offered the ability to alter the human race, to make every baby into a superman or a slave, into a genius or a moron. On demand. Pay your money and take your choice.

The world government was humane. And very human. Its leaders decided such power would be too tempting, too easy to corrupt. So, as humanely as possible—but with thorough swiftness—they arrested all the scientists who were involved in genetic engineering and exiled them to the satellite. Their knowledge was never to be used to alter the precious, hard-won peace and stability of Earth.

It had been Dan Christopher's father—with the help of Larry's father—who worked out the idea of turning their satellite prison into a starship. The Earth's government agreed, reluctantly at first, but then with growing enthusiasm. Better to get rid of the troublesome scientists completely. Let them go toward Alpha Centauri. Whether they make it or not, they will no longer bother the teeming, overcrowded Earth.

But the ship itself was overcrowded. Twenty thousand people can't be kept alive for year after year, decade after decade, for half a century or more. Not on a spacecraft. Not on the ship. So most of the people were frozen in cryogenic deepsleep, suspended animation, to be reawakened when they reached Alpha Centauri, or when they were needed for some special reason. The ship was run by a handful of people—no more than a thousand were allowed to be awake and active at one time.

All this Larry knew from the history tapes. Much of it he had learned side by side with Dan, his best friend, when they were kids studying together. Both their mothers had died of a virus infection that killed hundreds of people before the medics figured out a way to stop it. Their fathers had handed the infant sons over to friends to be raised, and went into cryogenic sleep, to be awakened when they reached their destination.

If they made it.

The people who had built this ship were engineers of Earth. The people who lived in it, riding out to the stars, were mostly scientists and their children. The ship had to operate for more than fifty years, if they were all to stay alive. The time was almost over, and the ship's vast intricate systems were starting to break down, to fail. Youngsters trained as engineers and technicians had all the learning that the tapes could provide. But could they keep the ship going indefinitely?

A month ago it was the main power generator that

failed, and they began to ration electrical power. Last week it was a pump in the hydroponics section; if they hadn't been able to repair the pump they would have lost a quarter of their food production, plus the even more important oxygen-recycling ability of the green plants that grew in the long troughs of chemical nutrients. And now the fire. Fifty people dead.

Will any of us make it?

A soft tapping at his door. Fingernails on plastic. Valery.

"Come in," Larry said, getting up from his chair.

The door slid open and she stood there framed in the light from the corridor.

Valery looked small, but she was actually almost Larry's height, and he had known since their childhood together that she was as tough and supple as plastisteel. Her face was broad, with high Nordic cheekbones and wide, always-surprised-looking eyes. Changeable eyes: sometimes blue, sometimes green, sometimes something else altogether. Very fair skin with a scattering of freckles. Very, very pretty.

She was wearing a simple white jumpskirt and blouse. Like most of the girls aboard the ship, Valery made her own clothes.

"I heard about your father," she said, her voice low.

Without waiting for him to say anything, she stepped into the compartment. Automatically, the door slid shut behind her. The room was suddenly plunged into darkness again. In the faint glow from the fluorescent painting, he started to reach for the light switch.

"No. . . ." she said. "It's all right like this. We don't need lights."

"Val—"

She was standing very close to him. He could smell the fragrance of her hair.

"I saw Dan. They took him to the infirmary. He collapsed."

"I know," Larry said.

He wanted to touch her, to put his arms around her and let her warmth engulf him. But he knew he couldn't.

"You'd better . . . sit down," he said.

Valery went to the plastic chair in front of the desk. She sat on it and tucked her feet up under her, as simple and feminine as a cat. Larry could see her in the darkness as a gleam of white, like a pale nebula set against the depths outside. He sat on the edge of the bunk.

"I wish there was something I could say," Valery began. "I just feel so helpless."

Larry found himself gripping the edge of the bunk hard with both hands. "Uh . . . how's Dan?"

"Asleep. The medics have sedated him. He's . . . he's not strong, like you."

"He does his thing, I do mine," Larry said. "He shows his grief on the outside."

"And you keep yours locked up inside you, so nobody can see."

He didn't answer.

"I can see it," Valery said, her voice soft as a star-cloud. "I came over to tell you. I know what's going on inside you, Larry. I . . ."

"Stop it!" he snapped. "You're going to marry Dan in two more months. Leave me alone."

Even in the darkness, he could sense her body stiffen. Then she said, "But I don't love Dan. I love you."

"That doesn't make any difference and you know it."

"You love me, Larry. I know that too."

He shook his head. "No . . . I don't. Not anymore."

Her face was lost in shadow, but her voice smiled. "Larry—remember when we were just six or seven and we snuck into the free-fall playroom . . . you and Dan and me? And we were playing tag, and you got racing so fast that you flew smack into a wall. . . ."

"It was the ceiling," he said.

"You hurt your shoulder, but you kept telling us it wasn't hurt. But I could see your pain, Larry. I could see it."

"Okay, so I broke my shoulder."

Suddenly she was beside him, kneeling alongside the bunk. "So don't say you don't love me, Larry Belsen. I know you do."

"It's no use," he said, his voice as cracked and miserable as he felt inside. "The computer selection was final. Not even the Council can revoke it. You can't have people just flying off and marrying anybody they feel like marrying! That's what happened to old Earth. The genetics went from bad to worse. We've got to live by the rules, Val . . . there's no other way."

"And the rules say I have to marry Dan."

"He loves you, Val."

"And you don't?"

He couldn't answer. Instead, he stared down at her for an infinite moment, then pulled her up to him and kissed her. She felt soft and good and loving. She clung to him hard, warmly. Everything else left his mind and he thought of nothing but her.

When he finally surfaced for air, she asked sleepily, "You don't have a duty shift, do you?"

Shaking his head, "No. Excused from duty until after the funeral services."

"Oh."

He sat there on the bunk, loving her and hating himself. *This is all wrong. What I'm doing . . .*

"Larry?"

"What is it?"

"If the Council would allow it, would you want to marry me?"

"Don't make it worse than it is, Valery."

"But would you?"

"Sure."

She sat up beside him. "We can do it, you know. If you really want to."

"You must be . . ."

"No, we can," she insisted. "The Council's due to vote on the new Chairman in two days, right? The Chairman and the permanent Council members are class A, aren't they? Their genetic options are much wider than B's, aren't they?"

"Yes, but . . ."

"I checked it all out. The computer selection rated you and Dan so close together that it wasn't until the third-order effects were taken into account that it rated Dan ahead of you. And then it was only a shade. But if you're elected Chairman, then . . ."

Larry shook his head. "It's Dan's turn to be Chairman. He's a year older than I am. Besides, he wanted to revive his father when we got to Centauri and turn the Chairmanship over to him."

"But that's all changed now."

Larry frowned. "No . . . Dan and I talked it over a long time ago. He's a year older than I am, so he'll get a chance to be Chairman first. . . ."

Very softly, Valery said, "That means in two months I'll be Mrs. Christopher. Unless you do something about it *now.*"

"I can't. . . ."

"Dan's in no condition to run the Council," she said. "When they vote, two days from now, he'll still be in the infirmary. And a lot of the older Council members have always thought he's much too emotional to be Chairman, even if it's only for a couple of months. Especially now, when we're about to make landfall . . . they'd rather have a stronger, cooler Chairman. You can ask my father; that's what they're saying."

Larry knew. He knew all of it. *To be Chairman when we reach the new world.* Every eligible young man and woman aboard wanted that honor.

"Do you think Dan could handle that responsibility?" Valery asked, sliding a hand around the back of Larry's neck.

Not as well as I can, he answered silently.

"As Chairman, you can marry me," she said.

"Val . . ."

"Don't send me to Dan. Please. It's you I want."

I CAN do a better job than he would. And marry Val.

"Larry, do I have to beg you?" She leaned her cheek against his. It felt wet. Tears.

"But it's wrong," he muttered. "It's like kicking my best friend when he's down."

"It's the only chance you've got, Larry. We all need you, everybody aboard the ship. You're the best one to be Chairman, everybody knows that. And I need you! I can't live without you!"

He closed his eyes and heard himself saying, "All right. I'll do it. I'll do it."

Chapter 3

The ship was built on the principle of wheels within wheels. It consisted of seven ring structures, starting from a central bulbous hub. Going outward, each ring was bigger and held more room for equipment and living space. The entire ship was turning, revolving slowly, to provide an artificial gravity. The outermost wheel, level one, was at one full Earth g, and everyone felt his normal Earth weight there. Going "upward," toward the hub, weight and gravity fell off consistently, until at the hub itself, there was effectively no gravity, weightlessness.

The thousand or so people who were awake and active had their living quarters in level one. All the levels were linked by tubes.

The infirmary was on the second level, where the spin-induced gravity was slightly less than 1 g. It made for an unconscious buoyant feeling, a sense of well-being and optimism, that the medics claimed helped to get patients recovered from their ailments.

The infirmary stretched over a long section of the second level. Instead of viewports looking outside, the main wall of the infirmary was made up of viewscreens that showed constantly changing pictures of Earth; old Earth, before the bursting population had torn down most of her forests, ripped open her mineral-rich lands, covered vast stretches of ground with festering cities.

Dan Christopher was sitting up in his infirmary bed, floating lightly on the liquid-filled mattress. He had drifted in and out of sleep several times this morning. When he had first been awakened for his morning check by the automated sensor system at his bedside, the scene on the wall screens outside his plastiglass-walled cubicle had shown an impossible blue sky and a vista of rugged white mountains dotted by patches of green, under a gleaming sun.

Dan knew that the sun was a star, but it didn't look like any star he had ever seen. Now, later in the morning, the scene was a deep green forest, where the sunlight filtered down in dusty shafts and strange four-legged animals tip-toed warily through the underbrush.

Wasting electrical power to show these scenes, he told himself. Dan still felt woozy, as much from the medicines they had been filling him with as from the dreams that haunted his sleep. The medics had pumped him full of tranquilizers, he guessed. But underneath their flat calming effect he knew there was a core of terror and rage inside him.

He's dead. The man who gave us this ship, the man who started this mission, the man who gave me life. The most important man aboard. Dead. A couple of months before we're due to reach our destination. A couple of months before he'd be reawakened and I'd get to really know him. Now he's dead.

Two nurses walked briskly past his cubicle, chatting together. Dan paid no attention to them. The chief medic would be here soon. Dan wanted to get out of the infirmary.

A tapping on his door snapped him fully awake. Through the plastiglass he saw Joe Haller: solid, dependable Joe. A good engineer and a good friend. Joe's long hair and beard turned off many of the older people, but he was one of the most reliable and brightest men aboard. Next to Larry, Joe was Dan's best and longest friend.

Dan waved him in, and Joe opened the plastiglass door and stepped into the cramped cubicle. There was no room for a chair, so he simply stood next to Dan's bed.

"How're you feeling?" he asked.

Dan said, "Good enough. I've got to get out of here today. How long have I been here?"

"This is the third day."

Dan could feel a shock race through him. "Three days? Then the Council meeting . . ."

"It's over. They picked Larry as Chairman."

"Larry!"

Joe shrugged and evaded looking straight into Dan's eyes. "Larry was there, you weren't. I don't know what went on before the meeting, what Larry did to convince them. The rumble is that Larry let them know he wanted to be Chairman, and as long as you were too sick to depend on, he ought to have the job."

Dan sagged back in the bed.

Looking worried, Joe added, "They . . . uh, they held services for the people who died in the fire—yesterday."

"Yesterday."

"Yeah."

"My father too? They didn't wait . . ."

"Everybody. One single service. Their remains went into the hydroponics tank."

"They couldn't wait for me?"

Joe shrugged and looked away.

Dan reached up and grabbed his wrist. "They couldn't wait a day or two for me to be there?" he shouted. "For my own father!"

"Larry decided . . ."

"Larry!"

"Listen," Joe said, his voice suddenly low and urgent. "I know you and Larry have been friends since you were kids. But he sure isn't acting like a friend of yours right now."

Dan let himself sink slowly back into the yielding warmth of the bed again. He could feel his heart racing. Deliberately, he took a deep, calming breath.

"I've got to be calm," he said, his voice steady now. "If I get excited, the medics will trank me again. If I show them I'm calm and relaxed, then they'll let me out."

Joe looked at him for a moment. "What're you going to do when you get out?"

"I don't know," Dan said. "Something . . . but I don't know what."

Joe left shortly afterward. Dan held himself rigidly under control, not speaking, not moving, trying to not even think. He concentrated on the sensor screens next to his bed. Keep those luminous traces as calm and steady as you can. Watch them wiggle across the screens: heartbeat, blood pressure, alpha wave, respiration, basal metabolism. Calm and steady. Calm and steady. Stare at them, let them hypnotize you. *Feel* your heart muscle working inside you. Slower. Slower. Calm. Steady.

He fell asleep watching the screens. And he dreamed. Dreamed of the luminous lines worming across the screens; they were ropes, they were snakes, twining around him, choking him, crushing him. But then he was watching from somewhere far off as the glowing snakes squeezed the life out of someone else. His father! Himself!

He woke screaming.

"The more I think about it, the more glad I am that we voted you Chairman," said Dr. Loring.

Larry Belsen was sitting in the main room of the Lorings' quarters. Valery sat next to him on the foldout couch. Her father was comfortably sunk in the depths of a webchair. Every time he moved, the plastic webbing creaked; Larry was afraid it would give way under his weight.

Dr. Loring was one of the twelve oldest men awake, and thus was a permanent member of the Council. He had been a child when the ship had left Earth, and had never undergone deepsleep. "I want to see it all, from beginning to end," he often said. The Council balanced age, tradition and stability against youth, vigor and change. The twelve oldest people awake were permanent members. The remaining Council seats were filled by younger men and women, and the Chairman was always elected from the younger generation, for a one-year term.

"Yes, you'll be a good Chairman, Lawrence, my boy," Dr. Loring went on. "Frankly, I always had my doubts about Dan . . ." he glanced at his daughter, ". . . as far as being Chairman is concerned. Too emotional. That's not bad in some aspects of life, of course, but as Chairman . . ."

Valery smiled at the old man. "Dad, you've told us the same thing three times now."

"Oh? Really? Well . . ." He shook his head, looking slightly embarrassed. Dr. Loring was a heavy man, big-boned and round with paunch. He was nearly bald, nothing but scraggly white tufts of hair sticking out around his ears. His eyes were big and moist and always blinking. Larry thought of him sometimes as a frog who'd been turned into a prince . . . fifty years ago.

Dr. Loring turned in his webchair, producing a chorus of groans from the plastic, and called to his wife: "What about dinner?"

She was standing in the kitchen alcove, thoughtfully watching the bank of dials set alongside the eye-level oven.

"I'm trying to time everything so that it's all done together, and everything will be hot when we sit down. . . . Valery, you can fold out the table and set places."

As Val got up, Dr. Loring complained, "It was a lot easier when the microwave ovens were working. This business of using heat for cooking . . . it's barbaric."

Larry said, "We just can't afford the electrical power for microwave cooking until the main generator's back on the line."

"Hmmph. There's another thing about Dan. How long has that generator been out? It's his responsibility. . . ."

"Now don't go blaming him," Larry said strongly. "It's

not his fault. Nobody aboard ship knows much about the generator. . . . Dan's had to train himself and a special crew just to get ready to tackle the job."

Dr. Loring mumbled, "Well, it's been a long-enough time, certainly."

"They've got to be very careful," Larry insisted. "Joe Haller's going through the computer core for instructions about the generator. If they goof, you know, we'll be in real trouble."

"Don't get so upset, dear," Mrs. Loring said. "Dinner's ready at last . . . I think," she added.

The meal was fine. The vegetables and fruits came from the ship's hydroponics gardens; the synthetic meat came from the biochemists' "ranch," where nutrients and enzymes and other special chemicals were put together to form a constantly-growing blob that had all the nourishment of real organic protein. No one awake had ever tasted actual meat from a real animal, except in dimly remembered childhood, but the biochemists insisted that their synthetics tasted "just like steak . . . even better."

Larry found that he was getting more and more nervous as the meal went on. *Got to tell them about us sooner or later,* he kept saying to himself. But the dinner-table conversation kept rolling along, and he couldn't find an excuse to bring the subject around to himself and Valery.

He kept glancing at Valery, waiting for her to say something, to help him get started. But she looked more amused at his consternation than anything else.

As usual, Dr. Loring was doing most of the talking. Ordinarily, Larry could let the old man's rambling speeches go in one ear and out the other; but tonight he was getting edgy. *Damn, I wish he'd shut up for a minute!*

It was Mrs. Loring who finally came to his rescue. She was the model from which Valery got her looks. Even at her age, she still looked lovely, strong, vital. Her hair was still the same sun-gold as Valery's; her eyes sparkled the same way.

She laid a hand on her husband's arm and said, interrupting him, "Dear, why don't we have some wine with our dessert? Is there still some left in that bottle you made?"

He looked at her, puzzled, for a moment. "H'mm? Uh, why yes . . . but . . ."

"I know we save it for special occasions," Mrs. Loring said, "but this is a special occasion, isn't it? After all, it's not every day that we elect a new Chairman."

As Dr. Loring pushed his chair back from the table, Larry took the opportunity:

"It's a double occasion. . . . Valery and I want to get married." He said it as quickly as he could.

"What? Married . . ." Dr. Loring blinked at him.

Mrs. Loring didn't seem surprised at all. "Why, that's marvelous. And now that you're Chairman, you don't have to be hemmed in by all those silly computer rules, do you?"

Dr. Loring broke into a huge grin and grabbed Larry's hand. Pumping it hard enough to shake the table, he said heartily, "Congratulations. I'm very glad . . . *very* glad!"

Larry felt a thousand kilos lighter. He looked at Valery. Her mother kissed her cheek. They were both beaming.

"The wine," Dr. Loring said, finally letting go of Larry's hand. "Yes, by heaven, this *is* a special occasion." He got up from the table and waddled back toward the kitchen alcove. Opening a closet door, he muttered, "It's in here someplace."

"I'm very happy for the two of you," Mrs. Loring said quietly. "I know that Valery thinks the world of Dan—but you were her first choice."

Larry grinned foolishly, but inwardly he was thinking about Dan. *First the Chairmanship, now Valery. He's going to hate me. And I don't blame him.*

Valery said, "I've been thinking . . . maybe it would be best if we didn't tell Dan about . . . us. Not yet. He's upset enough right now."

Mrs. Loring nodded. "Yes, you're right."

"I don't know . . ." Larry started to object.

Valery turned to him and smiled her prettiest. "Please, Larry. It wouldn't be fair to Dan to hit him with this. Not just now."

"But it's not fair to let him think . . ."

"Let me handle it," she said.

"Well . . ."

"Please?"

He melted. "All right. But don't let him think the wrong thing for too long. It'll just get worse, the longer we wait."

"I know how to handle him," Valery said.

Dr. Loring pulled a green bottle from the bottom of the closet. "Ahah!" He held the bottle up by the neck. "Not much left, but enough to toast the happy couple."

Larry smiled, even though he didn't feel particularly happy at that moment.

Chapter 4

Dan Christopher floated in nearly perfect weightlessness in the bulbous plastiglass observation blister at the ship's hub.

There was no up and down; or rather, any direction could be up or down, depending on your own point of view. At the moment, Dan was gazing out at a particularly bright star. It stood out among the millions of stars that were sprinkled like gleaming powder across the infinite black of space. Looking closely at it, Dan could see that it was actually two stars: the two main members of the triple star system, Alpha Centauri. Their destination.

Far, far behind the ship—nearly forty trillion kilometers, if you were silly enough to express interstellar distance that way—lay the sun, and Earth.

It was cold in the observation blister. The death-cold of emptiness seeped through the plastiglass. Dan pulled his electrically heated robe tighter around him.

"The dreams," he muttered to himself. "If only I could stop the dreams."

He had told no one about them. The medics hadn't wanted to release him from the infirmary, but he had argued them into it. He was perfectly healthy, except for the dreams. And in the week since his father's death, he had steeled himself to dream without screaming, without even tossing in his sleep. *Your mind controls your body,* he told himself. *Your mind can make your body do anything.*

All the anger and terror was buried inside him now, seething inside. But no one could tell it was there, not even the medics, although they hadn't been happy about releasing him.

Dan heard a hatch sigh open behind him. He turned, and in the dimness of the blister's anti-reflection lights, made out the sturdy form of Joe Haller. He was upside-down as he came through the hatch. He drifted that way in midair as he floated toward Dan, slowly righting himself in the last few meters as he approached.

"So this is where you are," Joe said.

"This is where I am."

"I went to see you at the infirmary, but they told me you'd been released. I've been searching the ship for an hour. . . ."

"I came up here to think," Dan said quietly.

"Geez, it's cold in here . . . wish we could get the main generator back on the line. We're going to need it when we get to Alpha C."

"Will the work be done by then?"

"Think so . . . if we don't run into any major snags."

Dan nodded. Then, "What caused the generator's failure? Have you found that out yet?"

"Old age, more'n anything else. You just don't run a machine for fifty years without wearing it out. Even if it doesn't have any moving parts."

"Wasn't it overhauled regularly?"

"Sure . . . but still, some of the electrical connections and the insulation hasn't been changed since day one."

Dan thought for a moment, then asked, "Is there any evidence of . . . tampering?"

"Tampering?"

"Deliberate damage. Sabotage."

Even in the dim lighting, he could see Joe's mouth hang open. "Sabotage? Who in hell would do a thing like that?"

"You found no evidence."

"Nobody looked for any. We're just in there to get the damned thing fixed, not play detective."

"Then the generator could have been deliberately knocked out."

Joe shook his head, a motion that made his body drift away slightly in the zero gravity. "Who'd want to do that? It's like slitting your own throat. We all need that electrical power. . . ."

Dan turned away from him and looked back at the stars. At the double star, close, beckoning.

"One thing leads to another," he said. "The generator blows out. This puts an extra load on the auxiliary power units. The circuits in the cryonics section overheat. A fire starts. My father dies. I get hospitalized. The Council elects a new Chairman. . . ."

"Do you realize what you're saying?" Joe's voice was barely audible, shocked.

Dan nodded grimly. "That's why I'm speaking softly, and saying it here, and only to you. If I had anything

more than a few bad dreams, a few ugly thoughts—I'd be
screaming it over the intercom system and going after the
murderers with any weapon I could lay my hands on."

"Murderers? Dan—that's crazy!"

"Is it? Is it really?"

Joe didn't answer, merely shook his head.

"In another two months we'll be in orbit around the
major planet of Alpha Centauri," Dan said. "Key people
among the cryosleepers will be awakened. My father—
who was in charge of this when the voyage started—
would have naturally resumed command . . ."

"No, the Chairman elected by the Council would be in
charge."

"I would have been that Chairman! But Larry's taken
it over. He took it while I was locked in the infirmary.
And after my father died."

Joe actually backed away from him now. "Dan . . .
you're accusing Larry . . . my god, he lost his father in
the fire, too."

"I'm not accusing anyone," Dan replied, barely control-
ling the heat he felt within himself. "Not yet. There's no
proof of anything. But it looks rotten to me, Joe, and I'm
going to find out if I'm right or wrong."

"How?"

"I don't know. . . . I'll need help. Your help."

"Doing what?"

Dan grimaced. "Watching. Looking for evidence. I . . .
could be all wrong, I know that. But—Joe, I can't sleep,
not until I'm certain that this is all a nightmare, or . . ."
his voice hardened, ". . . or, I find the proof and punish
the murderer."

"Murder," Joe whispered back to him. "Do you really think somebody aboard the ship could . . . murder?"

"I don't know. I wish I did."

Larry sat nervously at the head of the long Council table.

The Council members were filing into the narrow room, in twos and threes. Dr. Loring took his seat close to Larry, smiling at him. *Trying to make me feel at ease.* The permanent members were seated in the even-numbered chairs. The younger temporary members sat between them, heads of thick dark hair, or blond, or red, alternating with the grays, whites, and bald heads of the older generation. Of the twenty-four Council members, nine were women.

The table was almost filled when Dan Christopher and Joe Haller came in together.

Larry felt a flash of surprise go through him. Then he rose from his chair and went down along the table to Dan.

"Hey, it's good to see you back on your feet again," he said, putting out his hand. "How do you feel?"

Dan shook Larry's hand without enthusiasm. "I'm all right," he answered.

"I didn't know you'd be out of the infirmary today," Larry apologized. "I was going to visit you. I did drop in once, but they told me you were sleeping."

"I'm fine now," Dan said.

And sore as hell, Larry realized. "Look . . . uh, why don't we get together after this meeting and talk. There's a lot we ought to hash over."

Dan nodded. "Okay."

Feeling even shakier than before, Larry went back to the Chairman's seat and opened the meeting. He let the automatic procedures of every meeting smooth over his nervousness, and sat there listening to his pulse beating in his eardrums as the minutes of the previous meeting flashed on the wall screen at the far end of the long, narrow room.

They rumbled through old business, and listened to Joe Haller's report on progress with the generator. Adrienne Kaufman, head of the Genetics Section, recommended that the Council offer its official expression of sympathy for those who lost family members in the recent fire. Larry glanced at Dan while the unanimous vote was made; Dan was staring at him, his eyes ablaze.

Then came new business, and Larry heard himself saying:

"As you know, we'll be in the Alpha Centauri system in about two months. Our trajectory will bring us to a point where we fly-by the major planet. At some point before our closest approach, we must decide if we want to decelerate and take up orbit around the planet, or continue onward and out of the Centauri system. So it's time for us to begin a serious review of what's known about the planets and to consider launching our remote probes, to gather more data on them."

Pressing a stud set into the tabletop before him, Larry said, "Here's the best holo of the major planet that we have, taken by the original probe from Earth, nearly a century ago."

The wall screen seemed to dissolve. In its place, deep space itself took form, with stars hanging everywhere, and a fat, yellowish ball of a planet sitting in the middle of the emptiness.

"Dr. Loring, could you review what's known about the major planet?" Larry asked.

"Not terribly much, I'm afraid," Loring began in his most pedantic style. "That primitive probe was woefully small, and a horrendous communications problem— transmitting holographic data over more than four light-years is no simple problem, believe me! And, of course, the men who launched the probe weren't considering settling down on the Centaurian planets to live. In fact, they didn't even know there were any planets in the Alpha Centauri system when the probe was launched."

"All right," said one of the other elder Councilmen. "Now how about telling us what we *do* know?"

"Certainly, certainly," Dr. Loring replied. "I won't even discuss the minor planet . . . it's airless, bare rock, baked by the big star, Alpha Centauri A . . . which, as you know is almost exactly like the sun. I don't foresee any radiation problems for us from A . . . and star B is small and cool, no problems there either. No worries about high fluxes of ultraviolet or x-rays and such. Now Proxima—the third star of the system—is so dim and so far away that it will look like an ordinary star up in the sky. No influence on the planet at all."

"What about the planet itself?" Adrienne Kaufman asked sharply.

"Oh, yes . . . Frankly, it's not going to be paradise. The white clouds you see flecking the surface are water vapor, all right, and the temperature range of the planet should permit liquid water on its surface. But, as you can see, that surface is mostly yellow-green. Watery planets, such as Earth, tend to look blue."

"What is the yellow-green stuff?"

Loring shrugged elaborately. "I wish I could tell you. The spectroscopic data returned by the original probe was very scant. I've been doing additional work with our equipment in the hub, but it's still very skimpy data. There's no evidence yet of liquid water on the surface. The planet's density appears to be rather high, judging from the orbits of its little moonlets. Its surface gravity might be as high as 1½ g . . . certainly no lower than 1.2. Anyone standing on that planet is going to feel heavier than he does now by 20 to 50 percent."

"That could make life unpleasant."

The chief medic said, "It could make life impossible for us on the surface. Human beings can't live normal, active lives under a continuous 1.5-g load. It would ruin your back, your abdominal wall, your feet and legs."

"But the data's so sketchy. . . ."

Larry took over. "It's very sketchy, and it could be wrong, too. I think we ought to launch our own probes as soon as possible, and start to get more detailed and reliable information."

There was a general murmur of agreement.

Dan Christopher spoke up. "What happens if we find that the planet is as bad as we fear?"

Silence. Everyone turned to look at Dan, sitting down at the far end of the table, then one by one they turned back to look at Larry for an answer.

Larry hiked his eyebrows. "We'd have two possible alternatives. Either stay in orbit and live in the ship until we can raise a generation of children who are genetically altered so that they're suited for life on the planet's surface . . . or keep going and look for another star with a more Earthlike planet."

"Which would you recommend, in such a case?" Dan asked.

Larry sensed danger, a trap. "It's much too early to try to answer that question," he said slowly. "There are too many variables, too many unknowns."

Joe Haller said, "Truthfully, I wouldn't want to bet on this bucket of transistors making it much farther than Alpha Centauri."

"And we know nothing at all about possible Earthlike planets around other stars," Dr. Loring pointed out.

"Then we've got to stay at Alpha Centauri and modify our children to live on the major planet," Dan said.

Larry found himself shaking his head. "We don't know yet. There's a chance that we won't be able to do that, even if we want to. And to expect the rest of us to live out our lives here in the ship while we're raising children who'll leave us and go live on the surface . . . well, I think we might run into some psychological problems there."

"Wouldn't there be psychological problems connected with sailing off for some unknown destination?" Dan asked.

"Yes, sure, but . . ." Larry stopped himself. *Why does he want to start an argument?* "Look, there's no sense talking about this until we have some data back from the close-up probes."

Emile Polanyi, chief of the engineering department,

said in a deep voice that still carried traces of old Europe, "We can launch the probes after a few days' checkout. They are capable of high acceleration, and could be in orbit around the major planet in a few weeks."

"What about landing on the planet itself?" Dan asked.

"The probes are equipped with instrument packages that can be soft-landed on the surface."

"Good. We ought to begin the checkout at once," said Dan.

Only then did Larry realize what was happening. *He's trying to take the meeting away from me. He's trying to show everyone that he's in charge, no matter who they elected Chairman.*

Chapter 5

The meeting ended.

Much more swiftly than they had drifted into the meeting room, the Council members cleared out. Larry watched them leave, all of them except Dan. Finally he was alone in the room except for Dan. They sat at opposite ends of the table staring at each other.

I've known him all my life, Larry thought, *and now he's a stranger.*

He got up from his seat and forced himself to walk down along the table to where Dan was sitting.

"I guess you *do* feel okay," Larry said, putting on a smile. He sat on the edge of the table, next to Dan's chair. "You sure made yourself heard."

Dan was slouched back in his seat. He looked up at Larry and asked, "Why'd you get yourself elected Chairman? We agreed that I'd take it this year."

"I know," Larry said, feeling rotten. "You . . . well, you were laid up in the infirmary, no telling how long you'd be there. The medics kept saying you were okay physically, but emotionally . . ."

"So you stepped in."

"Yes."

"And being Chairman gives you the right to marry Valery, too, doesn't it?"

God, he can see right through me!

"Don't tell me that never entered your head," Dan insisted.

Keeping his voice steady, Larry answered, "You know we've both been in love with Val since we were kids. . . ."

"The Lorings raised all three of us. But we're not playing brothers and sister anymore. Are you going to marry Val?"

"That's . . . up to her," Larry said.

"She's promised to me!"

"Computer selection. That's not final."

Dan's eyes flared, but he said only, "You're willing to let her make the decision between us?"

"Yes."

"All right."

Larry felt the breath sag out of him in relief.

But Dan went on, "Have you appointed a board of inquiry to investigate the fire?"

"Board of . . . no, we have the report of Mort Campbell's Damage Control group. That's enough. What good would a board of inquiry do?"

Straightening up in his chair, Dan said, "The cause of the fire should be investigated. Fifty people died, and we should know why. Somebody's responsible; accidents have causes."

Feeling bewildered, Larry said, "We know why. The circuits were overloaded, the insulation gave. . . ."

Dan banged a hand on the tabletop. "I want a full investigation! With a formal board of inquiry. And I want to head that board. If you won't set it up, I'll call for it at the next Council meeting."

"But that would be like slapping Mort Campbell in the face. After all, he's in charge of Life Support. . . ."

"I don't give a damn about Campbell!" Dan shouted. "Will you appoint a board or do I have to get the Council to do it?"

Larry felt ice-chilled inside. *Another try to get the Council under his own control.* "All right," he said slowly. "I'll appoint a board. You can even be its head. But you won't find anything that hasn't already been found."

"Maybe." Dan pulled himself out of the chair and strode to the door without another word or a backward glance. The door slid shut behind him with a click.

Larry sat there alone in the Council room for several minutes. Then he went back to his own seat and punched out a phone number on the tabletop keyboard.

"Infirmary," said a pretty nurse. Her face was ballooned many times larger than life on the wall screen.

"Give me the chief psychotech, please."

"Dr. Hsai? I'm afraid he's busy at the moment. . . ."

"See if you can interrupt him, will you? This is the Chairman; I must speak to him right away."

"Oh . . . yessir, I'll try."

The screen went blank for a moment while a part of Larry's mind smiled a little. *Rank hath its privileges.* The features of a thin-faced oriental in his thirties appeared on the screen.

"Mr. Belsen, what can I do for you?"

"I'm sorry to bother you, Doctor, but this is important. I'm worried about Dan Christopher . . . he's acting . . . well, strange."

Hsai made an understanding face. "Yes, that is to be expected. He feels the loss of his father very deeply, you know."

"Too deeply, do you think?"

The doctor smiled. "To paraphrase a venerable adage: How deep is too deep?"

Larry hesitated for a moment, then decided to say it. "Deep enough to unbalance him."

"Ahhhh . . . I see. You feel he is unstable?"

"He's acting strangely, Doctor. Making veiled accusations. He wants to investigate the accident in which his father died. He talks as if he thinks somebody caused the fire deliberately."

"Really?"

"Really."

Hsai thought for a moment. "Well, I had planned to check on him within a few days. Perhaps I had better make it sooner. And deeper."

"I'd appreciate knowing what the results are."

"Eh, the doctor-patient relationship . . ."

"Yes, I know. But Dan can be a very influential member of the Council. It's important that I know whether or not we can trust his judgment."

"I see. Well, I suppose I can give you some feeling in that regard without violating any sacred oaths."

"I'd appreciate it."

"Very well, Mr. Chairman. I shall see him tomorrow."

"Thank you, Doctor."

Larry's office, as chief of the Command and Control section, was actually a cubbyhole set between the ship's bridge and the computer center. Barely big enough for a desk and a small wall-screen viewer, the office was well suited for someone who was frightened of crowds and open spaces—or for someone who hated to spend much time at a desk and preferred to be moving around the ship.

Larry went into his office and sat at the desk. Suddenly he was very tired. He ran a weary hand over his brow.

A tap at the door.

"Come in."

It was Dr. Loring. "I am interrupting something?"

"No, not at all," Larry said. "Sit down." He gestured to the only other chair in the room.

Loring's bulk seemed to make the walls bulge outward. He squeezed around the plastic chair and then plopped down on it. Larry winced as the metal legs seemed to sag.

"I wanted to congratulate you . . . you ran a good meeting, despite certain, ah—interferences."

Larry nodded absently. "You know," he mused, "I hadn't really understood until today how likely it is that the planet we're heading for *won't* be suitable to live on."

"Yes. That would be a disappointment."

"Disappointment?" Larry swiveled his chair around to face Dr. Loring directly. "It'll be a catastrophe. It'll mean rethinking the whole purpose of this voyage. Do we really want to stay at a world that's not like Earth, and change our children into . . . into something different from us?"

"Frankly, I don't see any alternative," Loring confessed. "We don't know of any better planets elsewhere."

"Well, we'd better start looking," Larry said firmly. "I don't like being put in a corner. I want to have some choice as to whether we stay at Alpha Centauri or not."

Loring looked mildly shocked. "You're serious? You would actually consider going farther?"

Larry nodded.

"But . . . everyone on the ship thinks that our voyage is almost over."

"I know," Larry said. "It might be just beginning."

Dr. Loring shook his head, making his heavy jowls quiver. "The people won't like it. They are not emotionally prepared for going farther. The ship isn't built to . . ."

"The ship can be repaired, overhauled. The people— well, the people will make the final decision, I guess. But I'd like them to understand the alternatives. Or at least to *have* an alternative to Alpha Centauri."

"We don't have the equipment on board to study planets of other stars from the ship. We can barely make out details of the major Centaurian planet, as it is."

"Then you'll have to build the equipment," Larry said. "You ought to be able to do that."

"In two months? I'm . . ."

"You've got less time than that," Larry said, his voice hard and cold as plastisteel. "I want to be getting some data before we're forced to settle into an orbit around the major planet."

For once, Loring was speechless. He sat there open-mouthed, blinking wetly.

"You'll get all the help you need," Larry said. "I'll see

to that. But I want evidence of other Earthlike planets. They've got to be out there somewhere."

"Why? Because you want them to exist?"

Larry could feel his teeth clenching. He forced himself to stay as calm as possible while answering, "No . . . it's not just that. I don't want to see my children altered to live on an inhuman world. Val's children. Your grandchildren."

Dr. Loring was silent for a long moment. Then, "He's called her, you know."

"Dan?"

"Yes. He wants to have dinner with her tonight."

"She agreed?"

"Yes. I expect she'll tell him about her decision to marry you."

With a shake of his head, Larry replied, "No, I don't think so. He's been through enough recently; I don't think Val will want to add that to his troubles."

"But she's got to!" Dr. Loring's face started to redden. "Otherwise . . . she can't let him think . . ."

"I know," Larry said. "I know. But I'm afraid that Dan's right on the edge of a real mental crackup. He's like a man who's gone outside and tethered himself to the level one wheel. He's spinning around and around . . . and the more he spins, the wilder he feels."

It had been a quiet, tense dinner. Valery and Dan had eaten in the ship's main autocafeteria, in one of the shadowy little booths far away from the main dining area and the pickup lines with their crowds and noise.

They had said very little. Val looked beautiful but very

serious in a red jumpsuit. Dan was dark and silent in a black coverall.

Now they were walking down a quiet corridor, back toward Dan's quarters, a one-room compartment exactly like Larry's. It even had one of Val's paintings on its wall.

"You've decided on Larry, haven't you?" Dan asked abruptly.

She stopped walking, right there in the middle of the nearly deserted corridor. "I think so. I told him yes."

He took her arm and resumed walking; she had to quicken her former pace to keep up with him. Without looking down at her, he asked, "You love him?"

"I love you both. You know that."

"But you want to marry him."

"He . . . he's asked me to."

"And you want your children to be the Chairman's son and daughter."

"No, it's not that!"

"And if I were Chairman?"

Valery shook her head. "You're not."

"I could be."

"No . . . not now. Larry has it and they'll re-elect him. You won't get another chance."

Still looking straight ahead, he asked, "Suppose he's voted out? Even before his first year's over?"

"What?" She stopped again and pulled her arm free. "What are you saying, Dan?"

With a shrug, he answered, "Chairmen have been voted out before their terms were up. When the Council decides that the Chairman can't handle the job. Or when they think there's a better man available."

"Don't try it," Valery said earnestly. "You'll be hurting Larry and you'll be hurting yourself even more."

"I deserve to be Chairman," Dan insisted. "But more than that—much more! —I want you. I love you, Val. I've always loved you. I'd tear this ship apart to get you, if I had to."

"Oh, Dan . . . don't . . . please . . ."

He reached out and took her into his arms. "You're not going to marry Larry or anybody else. Only me. You think you've made up your mind, but just wait. By the time we go into orbit around the planet out there, you'll see everything differently. You'll see."

Something in her head was telling Valery to push free of him, but something even stronger made her stay in his arms. Looking up into his intent, deadly serious face, she said, "Dan . . . don't make me come between you and Larry. You've been friends. . . ." It sounded pathetically weak, even while she was saying it.

"Larry might have murdered my father."

"*What?*" In sudden amazement, she did push out of his grasp.

"I don't think that fire was an accident. Somebody caused it. Larry benefited from it."

"Dan, that's insane! Larry's own father . . ."

"What'll you think when I prove it?" Dan said, his voice rising to nearly a shout. "Would you like to be married to a murderer?"

"Dan, stop it!"

"Well, would you?"

Valery turned suddenly and began running back down the corridor, the way they had just come.

"Val . . . wait . . ." He raced after her, caught her arm.

"I'm going home!" She pulled her arm free. "If you have any sense of decency at all you'll never mention such a crazy thing again. Do you understand? Not to me or anyone else!"

She left him standing there, looking suddenly alone and helpless—and yet, as Valery glanced back toward him, Dan also seemed darkly resolved, strong and purposeful. She shuddered. Larry, a murderer? It was insane. But . . . that meant that Dan was—insane!

Which was it?

And with a final helping of horror, Valery realized, *Whichever it is, I've helped to cause it!*

Dan watched her hurry down the corridor, knowing that he had driven her away.

Maybe I am crazy, he said to himself. *How could Larry . . . he couldn't, not Larry!*

But another part of his mind droned with remorseless logic: *Someone caused the fire. Someone killed fifty people and kept you from your rightful position as Chairman. Someone wants to change everything, have everything his own way.*

Feeling sick and confused and more angry with himself than anyone else, Dan made his way back to his own quarters.

It wasn't until he had dropped onto his bunk that he noticed his viewscreen had MESSAGE WAITING written in glowing yellow letters across it.

He sat up on the bunk and punched the yellow button among the cluster on the keyboard beside the screen. The face of a young man appeared on the screen. Dan couldn't quite place him; he knew he had seen him before, but didn't know him personally.

"I'm Ross Cranston, from the computer section. I have a private message for Dan Christopher. I'll be in my quarters until first shift starts tomorrow morning."

The taped message faded from the screen. Puzzled, Dan touched the green button and said, "Get me Ross Cranston, please."

The computer-directed phone circuits answered with nothing but a faint hum. Then the same face appeared on the screen.

He looked just a little startled. "Oh . . . you're Dan Christopher, aren't you?"

"That's right," Dan said. "You wanted to speak to me."

Cranston said, "Yes. But not on the phone. Are you busy? Can I come to your quarters . . . or you can come to mine."

"What's this all about?" Dan asked.

Nervously, Cranston answered, "I'd rather . . . it'd be better to talk in private."

"About what?" Dan insisted.

"Your father."

Dan was instantly taut with tension. "I'll come to your place. What's the number?"

Ten minutes later Dan was tapping on Cranston's door. Politeness dictated a light tap with the fingernails; the compartments were all small enough for that sort of noise to be heard instantly, and it didn't disturb the next compartment, just a few steps away. But something in Dan wanted to pound on the door with both fists.

Cranston slid the door open. He was much shorter than Dan: sandy hair, worn long; roundish face, too puffy for a young man but not yet really fat. Nervous, light brown eyes darting everywhere.

"What's this all about?" Dan said as he stepped into the compartment. It was like all the other living quarters, except that Cranston had covered its walls with graphs and odd-looking sketches that appeared to be printouts of computer-directed drawings.

Cranston gestured Dan to a chair. He himself pulled a large pillow off his bunk, let it drop to the floor, and then sat on it cross-legged.

"I'm with the computer section," he began.

"You said that on the phone."

"Yes. Well, earlier today we were running routine statistical checks, inputting those fifty deaths so the computer could keep its memory banks up to date . . ."

Dan felt his insides churning. "And?"

"Well . . . when we input your father's name, a special subroutine must've been triggered. We got a message."

"A message?"

Cranston nodded. "It's kind of strange. . . . I'm not even sure what it means. But I thought you ought to know about it."

"What did it say?" Every nerve in Dan's body was tightening.

Cranston reached lazily up to his desk, beside him. "Here, I had a paper copy made."

Dan snatched the flimsy paper scrap from his hand. He looked at it, shook his head, and looked at it again. It said:

PRTY SBRTN 7, PRM MMRY 2337-99-1

"It's gibberish."

"No," Cranston said. "It's just a shorthand that computer programmers used around the time when the ship began the voyage. I checked that much."

"Then what's it mean?"

"If I'm right—and I think I am—it means that there's a priority subroutine number seven, in one of the prime memory banks. Those prime banks date back to the beginning of the voyage."

"What do the numbers mean?"

"It's some sort of code index, to tell us where the subroutine's located."

Suddenly Dan's temper exploded. "Subroutine, code index, memory banks . . . what the hell are you talking about? Speak English!"

Cranston actually backed away from him. "Okay . . . okay, it's simple enough. It looks to me like somebody put a special priority message of some sort into one of the earliest memory banks in the computer. The message was to be read out only in the event of your father's death, because the computer didn't tell us the message existed until we told the computer he had died."

"A message from my father?" Dan's pulse was going wild now. "Could he have suspected . . . did he know . . . ?"

Cranston was staring at him quizzically.

Dan grabbed the computer tech by his coverall shirtfront. "You find that message, do you hear? Find it as quickly as you can! But don't tell anyone else about it. Not a soul!"

"O . . . okay . . . whatever you say. . . ."

"How quickly can you get it for me?"

Pulling free of Dan's grip, Cranston said, "I dunno . . . hard to say. A day or two . . . if I have to keep it a secret from everybody else, maybe a few days."

"Get it as fast as you can," Dan repeated. "And not a word to *anybody*. Understand?"

"Yeah . . . sure . . ."

"All right then." Dan got up and strode out of the compartment, leaving the computer tech squatting there on the floor, looking dazed and more than a little frightened, slowly smoothing his rumpled shirtfront.

A message from my father, Dan told himself. *He must have known what was going to happen to him!*

Chapter 6

The bridge crackled with excitement.

Larry stood at his usual post, behind the curving bank of desk consoles and the seated technicians who operated them. Viewscreens flickered, showing every part of the ship, the pulsebeat of every system.

For an instant the whole bridge was silent, the silence of tense expectation. Everyone was holding his or her breath; the only sounds were the faint whispering of the air fans and the slight electrical murmur of the consoles.

Larry stood rooted behind one of the techs, watching a viewscreen on her console that showed the long glistening cylinders of four automated rocket probes. A red numeral 10 glowed on the screen, down on its lower right corner.

"Still holding at minus ten seconds," the tech muttered.

Another tech, at the next desk, added, "All systems still in the green."

On the desk just to the left of where Larry stood was a viewscreen display of a computer-drawn star map. Dozens of pinpoints of light were scattered across it. Off to one side of the screen, one of the pinpoints was blinking. This represented their target, the major planet of Alpha

Centauri. It was moving across the screen, heading for a dotted circle drawn in the middle of the map.

Larry watched the map. The blinking dot reached the circle and stopped there.

"Acquisition," said the tech at that console. "We're in the launch window."

The numerals on the picture of the probes began to tick downward: nine, eight, seven . . .

"Launchers primed and ready." A light on a console went from amber to green.

". . . six, five . . ."

"Probes on internal power."

". . . four, three, two . . ."

"Hatch open."

Larry could see that the metal hatch in front of the probes had slid away, revealing the stars outside.

". . . one, zero."

"Launch!"

The four cylinders slid smoothly away and disappeared in an eyeblink into the darkness of space.

"Radar plot," a voice said crisply. "On course. Ignition on schedule. . . . All four of 'em are on their way!"

Larry didn't realize he had been holding his breath until he let it out in a long, relieved sigh. The technicians whooped triumphantly, turned to each other with grins and handshakes and backpoundings. The girls got kissed.

"They're off and running," one of the techs said to Larry. Neither of them knew where the phrase had come from, but it sounded right for the occasion.

He stood in the center of the celebrating crew, smiling

happily. *In another month we'll have close-up data on the planet. Then we can decide to go into orbit or fly past and head out-system.*

They were all standing around him now, clapping him on the back and laughing with him.

Larry threw up his hands. "Hey, I didn't have anything to do with it. You guys launched the probes. I just stood back and watched you. You deserve all the congratulations, not me."

They milled around for a few minutes more, before Larry finally said, "Okay, okay, you got off a good launch. Now how about the regular duty crew getting back to their stations. Don't want to give the computer the impression it can run the ship by itself, do you?"

They grumbled light-heartedly, but most of the techs returned to their desks. The few extra people who had been present for the launch drifted away from the bridge, out the two hatches at either end of the curving row of consoles.

Satisfied that everything was going smoothly, Larry went over to his own seat along the back wall of the bridge and relaxed in it. But not for long.

Dr. Loring pushed his way past the last of the departing launch techs and entered the bridge. Larry suppressed a frown as the old man stood there momentarily, fat and wheezy and blinking, peering at the console screens.

He knows no one's allowed up here without permission unless he's a member of the working crew!

Loring turned his frogeyed face toward Larry. "Ah,

there you are," he said, and lumbered over to Larry's seat. "Congratulations. I was watching on the intercom. The launch seemed to go quite smoothly."

Larry got up slowly from his chair. "Thanks. But . . . you know that the bridge is off limits for non-crew personnel."

Loring waved a chubby hand in the air. "Oh, yes, of course. I apologize. But I, ah . . . I have other reasons for looking you up." He glanced around at the techs, who were all busily at work with their backs to him. "Ahh . . . could we step into your office for a moment? This is rather delicate."

There were times when Dr. Loring amused Larry, and other times when the old man exasperated him. This was one of the latter times. *Stay cool*, he told himself. *After all, he is practically a father to you. He thinks he's got a right to butt in.*

Nodding, Larry led Dr. Loring through the door in the middle of the bridge's back wall. It opened onto a short corridor that linked the bridge with the computer center. Off to one side of this hallway was Larry's office. They stepped inside and Larry passed his hand over the light switch. The infrared sensor in the switch detected his body warmth and turned on the overhead light panels.

Larry gestured to the webchair and sat himself behind his desk. Loring sat down with great caution, lowering his weight onto the fragile-looking chair very slowly. The plastic squeaked.

"What's the matter?" Larry asked.

"It's about Dan Christopher," Dr. Loring said, looking troubled.

Larry waited for the old man to add something else. When he didn't, but merely sat there looking unhappy, Larry urged, "Well? What about Dan?"

"And Valery."

Larry automatically tried to hide the jolting shock that went through him. *Idiot! What are you afraid of? She loves you.*

Patiently, he asked Dr. Loring, "Okay, what about Dan and Valery?"

Shaking his head, Dr. Loring said, "She's seen him a couple of times now since the fire. Had dinner with him . . . alone."

"I know that."

"I told her that I didn't think it was right; nothing can come of it but trouble."

"Is that what you came here to tell me? Val's told me about it already. We're not keeping secrets from each other. There's nothing wrong with her having dinner with old friends. . . ."

"He still wants her, you know."

"I know." *I remember how I felt when she was promised to him.*

"He's asked her not to marry you until after we've decided about the Centaurian planet."

Larry nodded again.

"He's going to cause trouble."

Larry's patience was starting to wear thin. "Look, Dr. Loring, I know how Dan feels. I know he's trying to gain control of the Council and have me pushed out. But you've got to remember that he and I were friends for a long time and . . ."

"He believes," Dr. Loring said, his voice rising to interrupt Larry, "that the fire in the cryosleepers was no accident. He thinks his father was deliberately killed. Murdered."

"Murdered?"

"That's right."

"By whom? Who'd do such a thing? Why?"

Dr. Loring almost smiled. "You see, there are some things that you don't know. Valery's been afraid to tell you everything, for fear that it would cause more trouble between you and Dan. But I wormed it out of her. She can't keep secrets from her father!"

"Why in hell would Dan think his father was murdered? What possible reason could there be?"

Shrugging, Loring replied, "I happen to know that he has a computer technician digging through the oldest memory cores on the ship for some special instructions that his father fed into the computer—apparently when the voyage first began. Perhaps even before the voyage started, when the ship was still in orbit around Earth."

Larry sank back in his chair.

"Take my word for it," Loring insisted, shaking a stubby finger in the air, "Dan is dangerous. I think he's unbalanced . . . insane. And he's determined to get his own way—with the ship, with Valery, with everything. That means he's got to get rid of you, one way or another."

Dan Christopher's job aboard the ship was in Propulsion and Power.

Trained from childhood in physics and electrical engineering, Dan watched over the ship's all-important hydrogen fusion reactors, the thermonuclear power plants that provided the ship's rocket thrust and electrical power. Using the same energy reactions as the stars, the fusion reactors were small enough to fit into a pair of shielded blisters up on level seven—the innermost ring of the ship, closest to the hub. Small, yet these reactors had enough power in them to drive the ship across the light-years between the stars and to provide all the electrical power needed by the ship and its people for year after year after year.

The fusion reactors were like miniature suns. Inside each heavy egg-shaped radiation shield of lead and steel was a tiny, man-made star: a ball of glowing plasma, a hundred million degrees hot, held suspended in vacuum by enormously powerful magnetic fields. Deuterium—a heavy isotope of hydrogen—was fed into the fusion plasma almost one atom at a time. Energy came out, as the deuterium atoms were fused into helium. The same process that powers the sun, the stars—and hydrogen bombs.

There was enough energy in the fusion reactors to turn the entire ship into a tiny, glowing star—for an explosive flash of a second.

In theory, the reactors were expected to be quiet, almost silent. And the energy converters that changed the heat of the fusion plasma into electricity were supposed to be virtually silent, too.

Yet as Dan prowled down along the metal catwalk that hung over one of the reactors, he could *feel* through the soles of his slippered feet the low-frequency growl of a star chained to man's command. The metal floor plates vibrated, the air itself seemed to be heavy with the barely audible rumbling of some unseen giant's breathing.

Dan leaned over the catwalk's flimsy railing and peered down at the work crew on the floor below. The railing could be flimsy because the gravity factor at level seven was only one-tenth of Earth-normal g. The ship's designers had put the heaviest equipment in the areas where weight was almost negligible. People had to live at a full Earth g, so the living quarters were down in the outermost wheel, level one. But the big equipment was up here, where a man could haul a five-hundred kilo generator by himself, if he had to.

Dan could feel the frail railing tremble in his hands from the reactors' deep-pitched subsonic song. The reactors themselves were little to look at, just a pair of dull metal domes some twenty meters across: like a brace of eggs lain by a giant robot bird. Off on the other side of level seven was another pair of reactors, and the smaller auxiliary electrical power generators. Between the two blisters housing the big equipment was nestled the control instrumentation and offices for the Propulsion and Power group.

The work crew on the main floor below the catwalk was still trying to get the main generator going. All the repairs had been made, and the generator had been reassembled in its place between the two reactors. But it would still not light off.

As Joe Haller had put it after an exasperating week of working on the generator: "It's an engineer's hell. Everything checks but nothing works."

Dan knew they'd get it going sooner or later. But he couldn't help wondering why the generator wasn't working, when all the calculations and tests showed that it should.

Is there a saboteur in Joe's team? he wondered, watching them work. *And if so—why? Who's behind all this?*

"MR. CHRISTOPHER, MESSAGE FOR YOU," said the computer's flatly calm voice over the intercom loudspeakers.

Dan reluctantly turned away from the sweating crew beneath him and strode back toward the control area. The magnetized metal foil strips in his slippers clung slightly to the floor plates of the catwalk.

Shutting the door behind him, Dan felt the bone-quivering rumble of the reactors disappear, to be replaced by the higher-pitched hum of electrical equipment: monitors, computer terminals, viewscreens. A half-dozen people were seated at monitoring desks, watching the performance of the reactors and generators.

Dan spotted an empty desk, slid into its chair, and touched the phone button. "Dan Christopher here," he said.

The little desktop viewscreen glowed briefly, then Dr. Hsai's features took shape. The psychotech smiled a polite oriental smile.

"Kind of you to answer my call so quickly," Dr. Hsai said softly. "I know you must be very busy."

Dan smiled back. "You're a busy man, too. What can I do for you?"

Looking slightly more serious, the psychotech replied, "I am concerned that you haven't kept in touch with us, Mr. Christopher. We have set up three appointments for your examination, and you haven't shown up for any of them."

Dan shrugged. "As you said, I'm very busy."

"Yes, of course. But your health is of primary importance. You cannot perform your exacting tasks if you are in poor health."

"I feel fine."

Dr. Hsai closed his eyes when he nodded. "Perhaps so. But your condition may not reflect itself in physical symptoms that are obvious to you. You were discharged from the infirmary with the understanding that you would return for periodic examinations. . . ."

Dan could feel the heat rising within him. "Now listen. I *am* busy. And all you want to do is ask me more stupid questions and probe my mind. I don't have to allow that. I'm performing my job and I feel fine. There's no way you can force me to submit to your brain-tinkering!"

"Mr. Christopher!" Dr. Hsai looked shocked.

"Let me remind you of something, Doctor," Dan went on. "We're right now decelerating toward Alpha Centauri. Our reactors are feeding the ship's main engines on a very, *very* carefully programmed schedule. This ship can't take more than a tiny thrust loading—we're simply not built to stand high thrust, it'd tear us apart. . . ."

"Everyone knows this."

"Do they? This is a very delicate part of the flight. A slight miscalculation or a tiny flaw in the reactors could rip open the ship and kill everybody. I'd suggest that you stop bothering me and let me concentrate on my job. Save your brain-picking for after we're safely in orbit and the rocket engines are shut down."

"I am only . . ."

Dan could sense that the others in the control room had turned to stare at him. But he concentrated on the phone screen. "I don't care what you are only," he snapped. "And I don't care who's trying to find reason to slap me back in the infirmary . . . even if it's the Chairman himself! I'm going to stay on this job and get it done right. Understand?"

Dr. Hsai nodded, his smile gone. "I am sorry to have interrupted your very important work," he said.

The psychotech gently touched his phone's switch, and Dan Christopher's image faded from the screen. Dr. Hsai sat in his desk chair for a long moment, eyes closed, mouth pursed meditatively.

Chapter 7

It was late at night. Dr. Loring padded slowly up the long, winding metal stairs toward the observatory section in the ship's hub. The tubes that connected the lowermost rings of the huge ship had power ladders, and a man could ride comfortably at the touch of a button. Most people climbed the stairs anyway, because of the shortage of electricity while the main generator was down. But Dr. Loring felt it was his privilege to ride the power ladders.

Up here, though, above the fourth level, it was all muscle work. No power ladders, just endless winding metal steps. Not easy for a heavy old man. Even though the gravity fell off rapidly at these higher levels, Loring sweated and muttered to himself as he climbed. It was dark in the tunnels. The regular lights had been shut off, and only the widely spaced dim little emergency lights broke the darkness.

He stopped at the seventh level to catch his breath. Halfway up the next tube, he knew, he could just about float with hardly touching the steps at all. Time for a rest.

The hatch just to his left opened onto the Propulsion and Power offices, he knew. The hatch to his right led to the reactors. Loring wanted no part of them. With an effort he began climbing the next set of steps, leaving level seven below him.

"Insomnia," he muttered to himself. "The curse of an old man. Bumbling about in the dark, ruining my heart and my stomach, when I ought to be sound asleep in my own bed."

The weightlessness was getting to him now. No matter how many times he came to the observatory, the first few minutes of nearly 0 g always turned his stomach over. It felt like falling, endlessly falling. Something primitive inside his brain wanted to scream, and his stomach definitely wanted something more solid to work with.

If only it wasn't so dark, Loring thought. He held tightly to the stair railing as his feet floated free of the steps. At least he could keep some sense of up and down; that would help. Like a swimmer guiding himself along a rope, he pulled himself along the railing until his balding head bumped gently on a hatch.

Dr. Loring swore to himself softly, opened the hatch manually—the automatic controls were shut down—and floated through into the observatory.

For a terrified moment he thought he was outside in space itself.

The observatory was almost entirely plastiglass, a big dome of transparent plastic that made it look as if there was absolutely nothing between him and the stars. In an instant his fright passed, and then he smiled and floated like a child on a cloud, turning slowly around in midair to see his oldest friends:

Alpha Centauri, and 'way out there, I see you, Prox-

ima. The Cross and Achernar. He turned again. *How dim and far away you are, my Sun. And Cassiopeia, and bright Polaris . . . yes, still there. Eternally, eh? Eternally. Or close enough to it.*

Gradually, he became aware of dark shapes around him, blotting out parts of the sky. He knew what they were. Telescopes, recording equipment, video screens and cameras, computer terminals. The tools of the astronomer's trade.

He "swam" down to the desk that was shoehorned into the midst of all the equipment, and touched a button on its surface. The viewscreen on the desktop lit up, showing an intensified view of what the main telescope was looking at: the two main stars of the Alpha Centauri system, and between them, two specks of light that were planets.

Dr. Loring swiveled his chair around and activated the computer terminal. Its smaller screen stayed dark, but the READY light beside it glowed green.

Checking the time on his wristwatch, Dr. Loring stated the date, his name, and the code words for the computer memory section that his work was being filed under. Then:

"Re-position the main telescope for observation of Epsilon Indi."

The hum of electrical motors, and the bulky shape of the main telescope began to swing across the background of stars over the old man's head. Loring watched the viewscreen, and saw a bright orange star center itself in the picture.

"Analysis of last week's observations have shown," he recited for the computer's memory bank, "that both Epsilon Eridani and Epsilon Indi have planetary companions. Both stars are K-sequence, brighter and hotter than the red dwarfs observed earlier. The mass of Epsilon Eridani's companion is about one-hundredth of Jupiter's or roughly three times Earth's. This is a preliminary figure, and may apply to the total masses of several planets, although only one has been observed so far. The purpose of tonight's observation is to gain mass data on the companion or companions of Epsilon Indi. Spectroscopic measurements can be . . ."

He stopped. There was something moving among the shadows. The only light in the huge sepulcher-like observatory came from the dimly glowing viewscreen and the stars themselves. But something had definitely moved out near the main telescope.

"Who's there?" Dr. Loring called out.

No answer.

Annoyed, he raised his voice. "I know I saw someone moving out there. Now, I don't want to ruin my night sight by turning on the lights, but if you don't come out and . . ."

A hand on his shoulder made him jump.

"Wha . . . who . . ."

"You weren't supposed to be here," a voice whispered. "Old fool, you should have been safely in bed."

"Who is it? What . . ."

Loring caught just the swiftest impression of a hand swinging toward him, then his skull seemed to explode and everything went completely blank.

As the old man slumped in his seat, the lean figure standing over him bent down and felt for a pulse. Then he pushed Loring out of the seat. The astronomer drifted weightlessly off, bumped against the computer terminal desk, and slid gently to the deck.

The lithe dark figure touched buttons on the computer terminal. Dr. Loring's series of observations played out on the screen: all the astronomer's words, the notes he made, the figures he had the computer draw up, the tapes of the telescope pictures.

The figure touched one more button: ERASE.

The computer thought it over for a microsecond, then flashed a question onto its screen: PLS CONFIRM ERASE COMMAND.

"You don't want to be blanked out either, do you?" The figure smiled, and touched the ERASE button again.

WORKING, the computer flashed. ERASURE COMPLETED.

The dark figure nodded solemnly, then turned and picked up Dr. Loring by the collar of his coverall and dragged him lightly to the hatch. Opening it, he pushed the astronomer's portly body through. It floated down the tube, slowly at first, but as the gravity force steepened, it began to fall faster and faster. The dark figure watched as Loring's body flicked past the dim emergency lights.

"Dropping like a bomb," he murmured without humor, without hatred, without any emotion at all. "They'll find him three or four levels below . . . what's left of him."

Larry strode stiffly down the corridor, which was still shadowy in the dim night lighting. It seemed like an endless treadmill, featureless except for the doors on each side. The soothing pastel colors of the walls were faded to an undistinguished gray in the poor light. The tiled floor curved up and away in both directions, following the huge smooth circle of the ship's largest ring; it was uphill no matter which way you looked, although there was never any sensation of climbing at all.

But it looked uphill, and Larry felt as if he was straining up a sheer cliff wall. He didn't even bother to glance at the nameplates on the doors: he knew exactly which door he wanted.

He got there and stopped. With a deep breath, he tapped lightly on the door.

Valery opened it immediately.

"Larry, what is it?" she whispered urgently. "What's wrong? On the phone you looked . . ."

He still looked haggard, worried, deeply troubled.

"Is your mother awake?" he asked as he stepped into the Lorings' quarters.

"No, I didn't wake her. I think Dad's up at the observatory. . . . I heard him go out a couple of hours ago. He was trying to be quiet, but he can never . . ."

She saw the expression on his face and stopped talking. Now Valery looked alarmed.

"There's been an accident," Larry said.

Her mouth opened but no sound came out.

"Your father . . . he must've slipped and fell . . . down three levels of tube . . ."

"Oh no!" Val covered her face with her hands.

Larry went on in an emotionless monotone. "One of the camera monitors spotted him. We've got him in the infirmary—the medics don't think he'll make it. He's pretty badly mangled."

She collapsed into his arms. Larry held her and fought

down every impulse to relax his inner self-control. *Some-body's got to be strong. Somebody's got to keep his head clear. Can't give in to emotions. Can't relax. Not now. Not yet.*

So he was strong and calm, any sense of fear or sadness or guilt bottled deep inside him. He helped Val to calm down. Then they woke Mrs. Loring and broke the news to her. It took the better part of an hour before she was dressed, trembling and with tear-streaked face. The three of them went wordlessly to the infirmary.

Dr. Loring was in the same cubicle that Dan had been in. His body made a puffy mound on the liquid-filled mattress. His face was unrecognizable: half hidden in plastic spray bandages, half battered and discolored. Arms and legs were covered by plastic casts. Tubes ran from a battery of machines alongside the bed into his body, his nostrils, his head.

Larry glanced at the life indications panel above the bed: heart rate, respiration, alpha rhythm, metabolic level, blood pressure—all low, feeble.

Mrs. Loring collapsed. She simply fainted, and Larry had to grab her before she slumped to the floor. A pair of nurses appeared out of nowhere and took her off, muttering, "Shock . . . hypertensive . . ."

A medic came in a few moments later.

"I think it would be best for us to keep Mrs. Loring here, at least for the rest of the night."

Larry nodded.

"How's . . ." Val's voice was shaky. "Wh . . . what are the chances for my father . . . ?"

The medic tried to smile but couldn't quite force it

through. "We're doing everything we can. I think he's stabilizing—that is, his life signs aren't growing any worse, at least not over the past half-hour or so. But he's in very poor shape . . . he needs extensive surgery. It's probably beyond our limited capabilities. . . ."

Larry said, "There are expert surgeons in cryosleep, aren't there?"

"A few." The medic nodded. "I don't know the details of their backgrounds. . . ."

"I'll have them checked out. Maybe we can revive them."

"Revive them? That takes special permission. . . ."

"I know," Larry said.

"And the revival procedure itself takes weeks," the medic went on. "We'd have to suspend Dr. Loring in cryosleep until the surgical team could be made ready for him. I'm not certain he'd survive freezing, in the condition he's in."

Larry could feel Val's weight leaning against his arm. Without looking down at her, he told the medic, "Dr. Loring is a very important member of the Council, and as close to me as my own father. Closer, in fact. I want every resource at our disposal brought to bear to save him. I've already lost one father . . . I don't want to lose another. Do you understand?"

"Certainly, Mr. Chairman." The medic almost bowed. "Everything that can be done, will be, I assure you."

Turning to Val, Larry said, "All right. Come on, let's get out of here. There's nothing we can do except wait."

Slowly, he led her out of the infirmary.

As they walked along the curving corridor to nowhere

in particular, Larry said, "I want you to call a friend, somebody who can stay with you. I don't want you to stay alone."

"All right," she said quietly.

He glanced at his wristwatch: almost time for the morning shift to start.

"Larry . . ."

"What?"

Valery's face was pale, her eyes frightened. "It's like a sickness is sweeping through the ship, isn't it? The fire, and Dan's accusations, and now Dad . . . everything's going crazy."

For a few moments Larry didn't answer. The only sounds were the padding of their slippered feet on the floor tiles, their own breathing, and the vaster breathing of the ship's air circulation fans.

"Maybe," he said at last, "it *is* a sickness. Maybe there's a madman among us."

She should have looked surprised. But she didn't. "You mean Dan." It wasn't a question.

Larry shook his head. "I don't want to make accusations. Dan's been acting peculiarly since his father died, but that doesn't mean . . ."

"It's all my fault!" Val suddenly burst out, her eyes filling with tears.

"Your fault?"

"I've come between you. Dan hates me because I picked you, not him. He wants to get rid of you . . . destroy you! He thinks you killed his father, deliberately. And now . . . and now . . ." She couldn't speak anymore. She was crying.

And now he's tried to kill Dr. Loring, my foster father. Is that what she's saying?

The Council members were already in their seats, looking deathly grim, when Larry entered the Council room. The only empty chair was Dr. Loring's.

Taking his own seat, Larry said as unemotionally as he could, "I'm sorry to be late. I was in the infirmary. Dr. Loring is still alive, but just barely. The medics have decided to place him in cryosleep until a surgical team is revived for an attempt to save his life."

"If there is such a team among us," said one of the older Council members. "I don't seem to recall too many surgeons among our original number. Biochemists and geneticists, yes, plenty of those. But surgeons . . . ?"

Larry nodded curtly. "The computer is searching the personnel files for the right people. If they're found, I assume the Council is willing to waive the usual rules about retiring one person for each person revived? This is an emergency situation, after all."

They muttered and nodded assent.

"And if there is no surgical team capable of helping him?" Adrienne Kaufman asked.

"We'll just have to keep Dr. Loring in cryosleep until some of our younger members can be trained sufficiently well to operate on him."

"That could take a generation!"

"Once he's in cryosleep safely, it doesn't matter."

"The old man shouldn't have been wandering around the tubes by himself," said a young Councilman. "Accidents can happen to the best of us. . . ."

"Was it an accident?" Dan Christopher asked, from his seat at the far end of the table. "Seems to me we've been having far too many *accidents* lately."

"What do you mean by that?"

Larry wanted to say something, to take command of the discussion, but he didn't know how to do it without stirring Dan's antagonism even further.

"What was Dr. Loring doing up there," Dan asked, "at that time of night? What was he working on? His daughter tells me he's been spending lots of his time in the observatory on some special task. . . ."

A couple of the Council members turned to glance at Larry. *He would mention Valery,* Larry said to himself, trying to keep cold hatred from numbing his whole body.

"It's no secret," Adrienne Kaufman said haughtily. "Everyone knew that Dr. Loring was looking for other Earthlike planets, around other stars. At least, *almost* everyone knew." She stared icily at Dan.

"But there's no record of his work in the computer memory," Dr. Polanyi said. "I ran a check yesterday, when I first heard about the accident."

"It was no accident," Dan said firmly. "And his work was erased from the computer."

"What?"

"How can you say that?"

"It's ridiculous."

Dan leaped to his feet. "Ridiculous, is it? How'd you like to see *proof* that there's a murderer among us?"

Everyone started talking, arguing, shouting at once.

"*Quiet!*" Larry roared.

They all froze in mid-word. Arms stopped waving, voices hushed, and everyone turned to look at the Chairman.

Quietly, calmly, coldly, Larry said to Dan, "What's this all about?"

"I've been checking into the computer, too," Dan said, his dark eyes flashing. "And I've found something that shows there's an organized plot to undermine our whole flight . . . a madman's running loose, trying to kill us all!"

They all started jabbering again.

"Wait," Larry said, silencing them with a raised hand. "Dan, if you have such proof, by all means, let's see it. Right now."

Dan jabbed at a button on the small tabletop keyboard at his place. "You'll see it all right."

The wall screen at the far end of the room lit up and showed a human face. Louis Christopher, Dan's father, the driving force that made the ship, the voyage, their lives possible.

As Louis Christopher began to speak, Larry could think of nothing except the enormous likeness between father and son. The same long, lean, dark face. The same handsome features. The same intense, burning eyes.

"None of you will see this tape until I'm dead," Louis Christopher was saying. "The fact that you are viewing it now means that I have died. I hope that my death was a solitary affair, and hasn't affected the performance of our ship or the success of our voyage."

Christopher seemed to be staring straight at the camera, trying almost to hypnotize it, Larry thought. The effect was as if he was staring straight at the viewer, face to face.

"As I speak to you, our journey has just begun. Earth still looms large behind us. The stars are very far away. There are many among us who oppose this voyage, who think it's madness. Many among us were satisfied to remain aboard this ship in orbit around the Earth forever, prisoners, exiles for life.

"We voted to aim for the stars, though, and that's where we're going. Still, many are grumbling. They fear the unknowns of deep space. They're afraid of leaving Earth behind permanently.

"They may try to subvert our voyage. They may decide that they'd rather be exiles near Earth than free men among the stars. They may try to get us to return to Earth.

"That's why I'm making this tape. Since I must now be dead, it makes no further difference to me what you do. But it does make a difference to the future generations, to our children and their children. Continue the voyage! Don't let this magnificent ship, and our wonderfully brave people, be taken over by the fearful and timid. The stars are ours! We have the opportunity to reach Alpha Centauri and begin a new life there, on a literally new world. *Reject anyone who would do otherwise!*"

Several of the Council members shifted in their chairs. A few turned to glance at Larry.

"Our people have worked hard and struggled against titanic odds and risked everything they have," Louis Christopher continued, "to get to Alpha Centauri. We've pledged ourselves and mortgaged future generations yet unborn to make a new world for ourselves, far from Earth's decay and madness. You must continue until you reach that goal.

"Now let me point out another danger. It seems unlikely that the planets of Alpha Centauri will be exactly like Earth. We have, though, the means to adapt our children genetically to live on a different world. Don't be tempted to go further than Alpha Centauri. I know the construction of this ship, its limits and capabilities. It won't last long enough to reach another star. Settle on Alpha Centauri; to do otherwise will be to destroy the ship, the voyage, and every one of you.

"It won't be easy to change your children physically so that they can live on a strange world. But it must be done. It is the only way. Be strong. Be brave. Good luck. And good-bye."

The screen went dead.

For a long half-minute no one moved or spoke. Then one of the Councilmen coughed nervously, and they all turned in their seats, murmuring to each other. Dan remained standing by his chair, visibly trembling with emotion.

Larry said as gently as he could, "Is that what you call proof of murder?"

"What more proof do you need?" Dan blazed back. "*He* knew this would happen! He knew someone would try to subvert the whole voyage, push on to another star, get us all killed. He warned us!"

"But how does that prove he was murdered?" one of the women asked.

"Or that Dr. Loring's accident wasn't accidental?"

Glowering at them, Dan replied, "We all know that if my father were alive now, he'd be revived and we'd vote him Chairman."

Larry said nothing.

"And we also know that Dr. Loring was looking for another planet around some other star. If he had found such a planet he'd be blathering it all over the ship. He said nothing, because he couldn't find another Earthlike world. In fact, he must have found evidence for no planets, or hostile planets . . . because whoever tried to kill him erased his work from the computer memory so that we'd never know what he'd found."

Larry pointed toward Dan and shouted out, "Or he might have found a new Earth somewhere, much better for us than the Centaurian planet, and his would-be murderer tried to keep us from finding *that* out!"

They glared at each other from opposite ends of the table, wordless for a moment.

"This is getting us nowhere," Adrienne Kaufman said.

Larry took a deep, calming breath. "The truth of the matter is that there's no evidence of murder, not of anyone at any time. All the deaths and near-deaths that we've had can be attributed to accidental causes. And anyone," he stared right at Dan, "who insists on finding foul play behind every accident on this ship is running the risk of being thought insane."

Dan stood there, shaking with rage, face flaming. Then he spun around and stamped out of the Council room.

Larry turned to the chief meditech, who was sitting halfway down the table.

"I want him in the infirmary immediately. And I want him checked out even if you have to strap him down. We can't have a madman running loose aboard this ship!"

Because if he is insane, Larry said to himself, *maybe he is a murderer!*

Chapter 8

The cryonics room felt like gray November to Larry.

He had never known Earthly seasons, except through poetry and the videotapes he had watched during his school years. But here in the stark, cold, silent area where the frozen members of the ship's people slept away the years, he shivered with the incipient chill of winter.

The cryonics sections took up two full levels of the ship. The big compartments, called bays, were filled with row after row of massive covered couches, like the granite sarcophagi of ancient Egyptian pharaohs. But these coffins were for the living, not the dead; and they were made of stainless steel and plastic and honeycombed with tubes that carried liquid helium at 4.2 degrees above absolute zero. Instead of elaborate carved hieroglyphics, the cryogenic couches bore dials and gauges, automatic readout viewers that showed the condition of the sleeper inside. Alive. Frozen, unmoving, unbreathing, silent and still for year after year. But alive.

Larry had never been frozen. The prospect bothered him somehow. It was too much like death.

The entire cryonics bay was like death, like winter; cold, lonely, silent. His breath hung in misty clouds before his face, and he felt chilled to the marrow despite the electric jacket he wore over his coveralls. The glareless lights overhead made everything look even flatter, grayer. The softly padded flooring muffled even the sounds of his footsteps.

Dr. Hsai was already there, Larry saw. The oriental psychotech was waiting for him, several rows up ahead. Larry quickened his pace.

"This is a strange place for a meeting," Dr. Hsai said as Larry came up to him. He seemed more curious than upset.

"I wanted to talk with you privately," Larry explained. "This is one of the few places aboard ship where we can be sure of no interruptions or eavesdroppers."

The psychotech's thin eyebrows arched upward. "Ahh . . . just what was it that you wanted to discuss?" If he felt cold, Hsai wasn't showing it.

"I understand that you want to release Dan Christopher."

Hsai bobbed his head once. "There is no excuse for keeping him in the infirmary. He has been there for almost a month now. I have seen him every day. There is no evidence of mental abnormality—nor should we expect to find any, under these circumstances."

"What do you mean?"

"Mr. Christopher is not suffering from a physically caused abnormality. He is not schizoid, which is the result of molecular imbalances in the nervous system. Nor does he have any brain lesions, nor any other physically connected disease."

"But . . ."

Dr. Hsai raised a slim, long-fingered hand. "Please.

Allow me to continue. His problems are strictly emotional. Under the controlled conditions of the infirmary, this type of problem doesn't come to the surface."

Larry felt himself frowning. "But you can probe his mind . . . analyze what he's saying and thinking . . . his dreams and tests . . ."

"Alas," said Dr. Hsai, "I am only a psychotechnician, not a psychiatrist. Our only psychiatrist died in the epidemic a few years ago, you recall; the other two are here, in cryosleep."

"But can't you tell . . ."

"I can tell you that there is no physical reason for abnormal behavior in Mr. Christopher's case. His behavior in the infirmary was, at first, very hostile and suspicious. He was angry at being . . . as he put it, 'arrested and jailed.' But he adjusted to the situation within a week or so, and has been behaving very calmly ever since."

Larry muttered, "And there haven't been any accidents during the past month, either."

Dr. Hsai shrugged. "Either there is nothing wrong with him at all, or . . ."

"Or?"

"Or he is clever enough to hide his emotions from me, and he's waiting until he's released to work out his hostilities."

"Can someone be . . . well, can he act normal and still be . . ."

"Neurotic? Psychotic? Insane?" Dr. Hsai smiled sadly. "Oh, yes. The paranoids, in particular, can behave very normally . . . until they're placed in a certain stress situation. Then their psychosis shows up."

Larry shuddered, only partly from the cold. "What can we do?"

"It's doing no good to keep him in the infirmary. Frankly, he has every right to be released and resume his duties."

"But if we do, we run the risk of his going amok . . . causing more 'accidents.'"

Softly, Dr. Hsai said, "My own opinion is that there's nothing wrong with the young man, except anger and frustration. He feels the loss of his father very deeply; but even more deeply, he feels the loss of his expected position as Chairman and the loss of his chosen girl."

"In other words, he's sore as hell at me."

"Exactly."

"And he'll do whatever he can to get Valery back, and get himself elected Chairman."

"Yes."

Larry took a deep, cold breath. Looking straight into the psychotech's dark, calm eyes, he asked, "Do you think he's capable of committing violent acts? Like murder?"

Hsai shook his head. "Under the proper circumstances, anyone is capable of murder. Even you and I."

That's a big help, Larry complained to himself.

"He should be released," Dr. Hsai repeated. "You can have him watched as carefully as you wish, but there is no good to be accomplished by keeping him in the infirmary."

"All right," Larry agreed unhappily. "Let him go."

Hsai nodded and started walking away, toward the nearest hatch leading back to the warmth of life. He glanced over his shoulder once, looking slightly puzzled that Larry wasn't coming with him, or at least following him.

But Larry stood rooted to the spot, beside one of the bulky cryosleep couches.

Dan wants Valery, and he wants to be Chairman.

"You knew that," he said softly to himself. "That's nothing new."

Yes, his mind echoed back. *But if he is insane, if he has done all these crazy things—including murder—then it's because of me. The blame is partly mine. Maybe almost entirely mine. Especially if he's insane. Then he's not responsible for his actions. But I am. I am!*

"All right, so it's at least partially your own fault. What can you do about it now?"

He wanted to answer, *Nothing.* But instead he knew, *You can give him what he wants. Let him have the Chairmanship. Let him have Valery.*

"You know you can't do that. Not if you want to stay sane. Not if you want to go on living."

You can sleep. Right here. Sleep for as long as you want to. Sleep until they're both dead. Then start a new life.

"Sure. Or maybe never wake up."

It's your choice.

With a sudden shock, Larry realized he was standing in front of Dr. Loring's cryosleep unit. The graphs showed that the old man was still alive, waiting in frozen limbo for a surgical team to be organized for the attempt to save his life.

Give up the Chairmanship? Give up Valery?

"No."

*Then you'll be pushing Dan even further. He might do
something even worse.*

Larry was sweating now. Despite the cold, beads of
sweat were trickling down his face. "I can't do it!" he
whispered fiercely. "I won't let him have his way! I
won't!"

It was always noisy in the main cafeteria. Big enough to
handle three hundred people at a sitting, the cafeteria
doubled as an eating place, an entertainment center, and
an auditorium. It was brightly lit, gaily decorated, and
bustling with crowds nearly all the time. One entire wall
was a long viewscreen that showed constantly changing
scenes from Earth, from outside in starry space, or from
inside the ship itself.

At the moment Dan entered the cafeteria's big double
doors and stood blinking in the entryway, the long wall
screen was showing an ocean beach on Earth: surging
powerful breakers rolling up to smash against grim rocks
in spectacular sheets of spray. The sky was blue, the sun
a golden ball starting to turn red as it neared the horizon.
People dotted the tiny slice of beach that lay between the
rocks. Farther back, atop the higher rocky cliffs, there
were houses.

Dan stood at the entryway and took it all in: the video-
taped scene, the noise and brightness of the cafeteria.
After a month in the quiet confinement of the infirmary,
it was like coming to life again after being in cryosleep.

People jostled through the entryway past him. Several
of them smiled at him, or said some brief words of greet-
ing:

"Good to see you back, Dan."

"Hi, Dan."

"Hey, pal, how're ya doin'?"

"Can't keep a good man down, huh, Dan?"

He grinned at them, nodded, even shook a few hands.

Then he saw her far across the room, sitting by herself, looking tense. She had a tray of food before her, but she wasn't touching it; Valery was merely looking off into space, waiting.

Dan quickly made his way to the selector wall, punched buttons for the food he wanted, and went to the receiving slot. All the while he kept one eye on Valery's golden hair. He took his steaming tray straight to her table.

"I hope I haven't kept you waiting," he said.

She looked up, wide-eyed, almost startled. "Oh—no, I just got here a few minutes ago."

He sat down on the other side of the little table. "It was good of you to agree to meet me."

She seemed wary, almost afraid. "This is a funny place to meet . . . I mean, it's so noisy."

A group of half a dozen teenagers appeared on the stage at the other end of the room and started setting up electronic musical instruments.

Dan grinned. "It's alive. I like it. Kind of hard on the ears, but it's fun."

"You . . . you look very good," Valery said.

"You're scared of me," he realized. "Why? Do you think I'm crazy, too?"

"Who . . ."

He took her hand in his. "Come on, Val. I know what

Larry thinks. I know he's the one who kept me locked up for the past month."

Pulling slowly away from his grip, she answered, "Dan, I don't want you and Larry to be enemies. You ought to be friends again. . . ."

"I wish we could. I really do. I think I'd even let him keep the Chairmanship, if only I could be sure . . ."

"Sure of what?"

He shook his head. "It'd never work. You're the one I want, Val. If I had you, I'd almost be willing to let the rest of it go."

"The rest of it?"

"Yep . . . I had a lot of time to think, you know, sitting there in the infirmary. A lot of time. I understand there haven't been any accidents since I went in."

She hesitated, then admitted, "That's right."

"You see? He's been damned smart about it . . . damned smart."

"What do you mean?"

"He's trying to make it look like it's all my fault. Larry's got half the people on this ship believing that I'm crazy, that I've been causing the accidents, that I tried to kill your father."

She stared at him. "Did you?"

He looked back into her Arctic-blue eyes, sensing all the turmoil, the fear, the pain that lay behind them.

"Have you asked Larry that question?"

"What do you mean?"

"You know what I mean, Valery."

"But why?" she asked, so softly that he could barely

hear her voice over the cafeteria din. "Why would Larry do it?"

"Have you ever thought," Dan asked slowly, "that if there really is a madman aboard this ship, it's got to be Larry?"

"No! It couldn't be!"

"Couldn't it?"

"Dan—you're wrong. The accidents . . . they could be just that: accidents."

"Then why is Larry trying to prove that I'm insane?"

"He's afraid . . ."

"Afraid of me."

The words were gushing out of her now. "Larry's afraid that if you are sick, you'll hurt more people, hurt the ship, kill us all."

"That's just what *he's* doing."

"No . . ."

Dan could feel his temper rising, his face getting hot and red. "He's afraid of me because he knows that I know I didn't cause any of those accidents. He knows that I can't rest until I show everyone who did cause the accidents—who killed my father and nearly killed yours. *That's* what he's afraid of!"

Valery's voice was pleading, "Dan, listen to me. Believe in me. If you keep going this way, one of you—or both of you—are going to be killed! Stop it now. Let it stop."

He shook his head solemnly. "I can't, Val."

"Even if it means my sanity? My life? I can't stand by and see the two of you tear each other apart."

"There's nothing else . . ."

"Suppose," she said shakily, tears in her voice, "suppose

I tell Larry that I've changed my mind . . . that I want to marry you. Will you stop then?"

He felt suddenly as if he were in the zero gravity hub of the ship, in free fall, dropping, dropping endlessly, spinning over and over again, dizzyingly. . . . He squeezed his eyes shut. *Stop it! Stop it stop it stop it.*

Looking at her again, so intent, so beautiful, so afraid and lonely, he said, "Val . . . I don't want you as a bribe. It wouldn't work that way. We'd end up hating each other. I . . . no, it's got to be Larry or me. We've got to settle this between ourselves."

"You'll kill each other," she said, all the energy drained from her voice.

"Maybe."

"You'll destroy the ship."

"That's what I want to prevent."

"You—the two of you—you're going to destroy me."

And she abruptly got up from the table and ran out of the cafeteria, leaving him sitting there alone.

Chapter 9

For more than a month, the four gleaming torpedo shapes of the ship's automated probes had coasted silently through space, toward the major planet of the Alpha Centauri system. The only link between the probes and the ship was a continuous radio signal, of the lowest possible power, in order to conserve the energy of their batteries.

Then, as they neared the two main stars of Alpha Centauri, the solar cells along their outer skins began to convert sunlight into electricity. The radio signals gained in strength. Like sleeping servants, one by one the instruments aboard the probes awakened with the new flow of electrical power and began reporting back to the ship. But now the reports—full and complex—were carried by laser beams.

Some of the instruments took precise measurements of the probes' positions in space, and their courses as they approached the major planet. This information was studied by men and computer aboard the ship, and minor course corrections were transmitted back to the probes. The probes responded with the correct changes in course, and the men and women aboard the ship congratulated themselves. The computer accepted no congratulations, but took in all data impassively.

The probes successfully skirted past the steep gravity pull of Alpha Centauri B, the smaller orange member of the two main stars, and let the pull of Alpha Centauri A —the yellow, sunlike star—bring them close to the major planet. Then, more course corrections, more microscopic puffs of gas from the tiny attitude jets aboard the probes' bodies, and they fell into orbit around the planet.

Back on the ship, people celebrated.

Now streams of data began pouring across the near-emptiness of space between the probes and the approaching ship. The data were coded, of course, in the languages that the engineers and computers could translate into meaningful information. Pictures were sent, too, directly over the laser beams that linked the probes with the ship.

Two of the probes released landing capsules. One never made it to the surface, or at least never sent any information back after entering the planet's high atmosphere. The other touched down on solid ground and began sending pictures and data from the surface of the new world.

Larry was hurrying down a corridor on level two, where most of the labs and workshops were. Dr. Polanyi had been excited when he called: the first pictures from the planet were ready to view.

He saw someone heading toward him, from the opposite direction. The door to the data lab was halfway be-

tween them. Larry recognized the blazing orange coverall before he could make out Dan's face.

They had kept apart since Dan's release from the
infirmary. Now they met at Polanyi's door.

"Hello Dan," Larry said automatically, as soon as they
got close enough so that he didn't have to shout.

Dan nodded, his face serious. "Hello."

Larry reached for the finger grip on the lab door, but
found Dan's hand was already there and sliding the door
back.

"Polanyi called you, too?" Larry asked.

"He called all the Council members," Dan replied.
"Any objections?"

Larry knew he was glaring at Dan. "No objections—as
long as you can spare the time from your regular job."

Dan gestured for Larry to go through the doorway
first. He followed, saying, "The job's getting done. We finally got all the bugs out of the rebuilt main generator.
It'll go back into service today."

"That's fine. Glad to hear it." But Larry wasn't smiling.

"Ah, the first two here," Dr. Polanyi called to them.

He was sitting at a workbench halfway across the big,
cluttered room. The data lab was really a makeshift
collection of instruments, viewscreens, workbenches,
desks, computer terminals, and odd sorts of equipment
that Larry couldn't begin to identify. Half a dozen
white-coated technicians were tinkering around one of
the bulky, refrigerator-sized computer consoles. A wall-
sized viewscreen was set up next to it, on legs that looked
much too fragile to support it.

Polanyi fussed around the viewscreen and verbally

prodded the technicians. Larry saw that there were a few chairs set up, so he sat on one. Dan joined the technicians, watching what they were doing from over their shoulders. In about ten minutes, most of the other Council members showed up. The older men and women among them took the available chairs. Larry got up and joined the loose semicircle of younger men that formed behind the seats.

The technicians finally scattered to various control desks around the big room, and Polanyi turned to face his audience.

"You recognize, of course, that what we're going to see will not be holograms," he said. "There is holographic information in the transmitted data, but we have not deciphered it completely as yet. I thought it would be much more desirable to see what there is to see as quickly as possible, even if it is only a flat, two-dimensional picture."

Larry nodded and asked, "Are any of the views we're going to see from the surface?"

"Only the last three," Polanyi answered. "Data transmission from the surface has been very difficult, for reasons that we have not yet determined. The orbital data is quite good, however."

Larry suddenly realized that he had lost track of Dan. Turning and looking through the crowd, he spotted him, standing off to one side of the group.

The overhead lights dimmed out, and Larry turned his attention back to the screen. It began to glow. Colors appeared, forms took shape.

It was a still photo, taken from far enough away from the planet to show its entire sphere.

"This is the first photo the probes took," Polanyi's voice floated through the darkness. "Probe number one took this one, as you can tell from the numerals down in the lower right-hand corner of the picture."

The planet was yellowish. Broad expanses of golden yellow, dappled here and there by greenish stretches. Larry found that he couldn't tell which was land and which was sea. The entire planet was streaked with white clouds, which obscured much of the underlying terrain. But there seemed to be no major cloud formations, such as the huge storm systems he had seen on tapes of Earth.

"Next," Polanyi's voice called.

This view was much closer. Mountains showed as wrinkles, like a bedsheet that had been rumpled. The land was yellow, Larry saw. The green stretches weren't vegetation, they were water.

For more than an hour they studied the orbital photos. The planet had no major oceans, only a scattering of large seas. There were no ice caps at the poles.

Polanyi kept up a running commentary, explaining what they were seeing, filling in information from the other instruments aboard the probes. It all added up to a disappointing picture.

The planet was actually slightly smaller than Earth, but about the same density. Surface gravity was apparently one third higher than Earth's.

Somebody said in the darkness, "1.3 g. That means that a ninety-kilo man will feel like he's carrying thirty extra kilos around with him all the time."

"Like hauling an eight-year-old kid on your back."

"It certainly will strain the heart." Larry recognized the last voice as belonging to the chief meditech.

The air had slightly more oxygen in it than Earth normal, but also had dangerously high levels of nitric oxides and sulfur oxides.

"Volcanism," Polanyi explained, pointing to a photo of the planet's night side, where a series of brilliant red lights gleamed. "Active volcanoes . . . many of them. The infrared scans confirm it. The volcanoes are spewing out sulfur oxides and other harmful gases."

Larry grimaced.

The vegetation was a yellowish green. Chlorophyll was there, identified by the spectral readings from the orbiting probes. But the plant life obviously wasn't the same as Earth's greenery.

"What about data from the surface lander?" someone asked.

"Yes, it is coming up next."

The picture on the viewscreen suddenly changed to show a startling landscape. It was golden: yellowish plants everywhere, some of them thick and tall as trees, with ropy vines hanging from their arms. Yellowish sky, even the clouds had a golden tint to them.

"This photo was taken near local sunset," Polanyi explained. "I believe that accounts for the peculiar color effect . . . some of it, at least."

It was beautiful. Larry gazed at a golden world, with hills and clouds and soft beckoning grass of gold. Something deep inside him, something he had never dreamed was in him, was stirred by this vision. A world, a real world, where you could walk out in the open air and look up into a sky that had sunrises and sunsets, climb hills and feel breezes and swim in rivers. . . .

He shuddered suddenly. It was like self-hypnosis. This golden world was a trap. It was deadly. A man couldn't last five minutes on it, not unless he wore as much protection as he needed to go outside the ship and into space.

The picture changed. Now they were looking off in a different direction. The yellow grass and trees sloped down into a gentle valley. In the distance there were rugged mountains of bare rock, their tops shrouded in clouds.

"There are at least two active volcanoes among those distant mountains," Dr. Polanyi said. "The clouds themselves are mainly steam from the volcanoes."

It still looked so beautiful.

The picture changed again. It showed the view from the opposite side of the lander. The hillside swept upward, still covered with golden grass and shrubs. Up near the top of the hill, silhouetted against the bright sky, were four dark shapes.

"They appear to be animals," Polanyi's voice said. "From their distance, we have judged their size to be roughly comparable with that of an Earthly sheep."

It was hard to tell their shape. There seemed to be a head, the suggestion of rounded haunches. No tail was visible. You couldn't tell how many legs, because their lower halves were hidden in deep grass.

The overhead lights suddenly went on, and the picture on the viewscreen faded.

"That's everything we have so far," Dr. Polanyi said.

Larry squinted against the sudden glare. And found himself frowning. Looking around, he realized that he had spent his life in a prison. A jail. A metal and plastic confinement, breathing the same recycled air over and over again, knowing every face, every compartment, every square millimeter of space. Out there was a *world*. A whole broad, beautiful golden world that no one had set foot on, waiting to be explored, to be lived on.

Waiting to kill us, he reminded himself.

They were all murmuring, muttering, a dozen different conversations buzzing at once.

Then Dan's voice cut through it all. "So we have our first view of the promised land."

Larry stepped toward him. "It doesn't look very promising to me. A man can't live there."

"We can't," Dan shot back, "but our children could."

"If you make them capable of breathing sulfur and strong as a man-and-a-third."

"The geneticists can do whatever needs to be done."

Larry was about to reply, but caught himself. Instead, he said, "This isn't the place to debate such an important issue. I'd like to have a formal meeting of the Council tomorrow morning. We'll have to decide if we want to make this planet our home, or look further."

Dan said nothing. He merely watched Larry, with a quizzical little smile playing on his lips.

It was late evening. The corridor lights were dimmed. Larry and Valery had eaten dinner in the Lorings' quarters, with Val's mother. Now, after a long walk around level one, they were approaching her quarters again, strolling slowly along the empty corridor, hand in hand.

They came to an observation port and stopped. The port was an oblong of thick plastiglass. A padded bench ran along the bulkhead alongside it. They sat and for a long, wordless while gazed out at the sky.

The stars were thick as dust. One yellow star stood out brighter than all the rest. Nearby it, almost lost in its glare, peeped a dimmer orange star.

"Tomorrow the Council meets to decide," Larry said wearily.

"Do you think this is the end of the voyage?" Val asked.

He shook his head. "It can't be. We can't live on that planet . . . even though . . ."

"Even though?"

"It's so beautiful!" he said. "I saw the pictures from the surface today. It's so beautiful. If only we *could* survive there."

She asked, "Can't the geneticists . . ."

"Sure, they can alter the next generation of children so that they'll be able to live on the planet. But—the kids would have to be brought up in a separate section of the ship. They'd have to be put under a higher gravity, different atmosphere. The parents would have to wear pressure suits just to visit their own children."

"Ohhhh . . ."

"And what about the parents? Do you think people can stay aboard this ship, in this cocoon, this prison, and let their kids go down there to live? It won't work; the planet's beautiful, but too different from us. If we try to make it work, it'll tear everybody apart."

"Then we have to move on," Val said.

"Right. But Dan won't see it that way. He'll put up a fight."

"You'll win."

He looked at her. "Maybe. I wish I didn't have to fight him."

"He thinks the ship won't be able to go much farther," Valery said. "He's afraid we'll all get killed if we try to find another star, another planet."

In the dim light, Larry could see that Val wasn't looking at him, but gazing out at the stars. He reached for her chin and turned her face toward him.

"You've seen him several times since he got out of the infirmary, haven't you?"

"Yes," she said softly.

He let his hand drop away. "I don't think I like that. In fact, I know I don't."

"Larry," she said gently, "I'm a free human being. I can do what I want."

"I know, but—well, I don't want you to see him."

"Don't you trust me?"

He felt miserable, tangled up inside himself. "Of course I trust you, Val, but . . ."

"No buts, Larry. Either you trust me or you don't."

"I trust you." Sullenly.

"Well you shouldn't," she snapped.

"Wha . . . ?"

"Oh Larry—it's all so mixed up! I don't want Dan to hurt you. He . . . he said he'd almost be willing to let you stay Chairman if I'd marry him."

Larry felt his insides going numb. "And you said?"

"I . . . I let him think I'd do it, if he'd just forget about trying to hurt you."

He knew how it felt to have liquid helium poured over you: scalding cold. "You let him think that."

"I did it for you!"

"Thanks. That's an enormous favor. Now he knows that anytime he crooks his finger, you'll come running to him. All he has to do is start an argument with me, and he's got you."

"No . . . that isn't . . ."

Larry's hands were clenching into fists. "I must have been out of my mind to believe that you'd prefer me over him. You've always wanted him. Now you've got the perfect excuse to get him."

He heard her gasp. "Larry . . . no . . . please . . ." Her voice sounded weak, far away.

"All this time you've been letting me think that you loved me . . . it was only because Dan seemed out of it. But whenever he's around, you end up going for him."

"You've got it all wrong!"

He stood up. For an instant, staring out at the stars, he felt as if he could fall right through the metal and plastic wall and tumble endlessly into the cold of eternity.

"Wrong?" he asked in a near-whisper. "Do I have it wrong?"

And then she was standing up in front of him, her face suddenly blazing with anger.

"You two are exactly alike!" Val snapped. She didn't raise her voice, but now there was steel in it, hot steel that threw off sparks. "You think that you can own me. Both of you. Well, I'm not a possession. I'm *me*, and I'm not going to sit around here like some silly Earth flower while you two big strong men fight over me. From now on, you and Dan both can do without me. I don't want to see either of you! Do you understand?"

Larry staggered a step backward. "Val . . ."

"If you and your ex-friend want to battle it out, it will have to be over some other reasons than me. I'm not a prize to be handed over to the winner. You two can knock your heads together . . . I don't care anymore! I tried to save you, both of you. I love you both! Can't you understand that? I love you both, but I've always loved you best, Larry. *I'm* the one who made you go after the Chairmanship . . . because *I'm* the one who wanted you. But you're so intent on flexing your muscles and being jealous. . . . You're scared of Dan! And you'll never be able to be happy or free or yourself until you stop being scared of him. And the only way *that's* going to happen is for you to kill him . . . or him to kill you. That's what you're both heading for. But I won't have any part of it! Go ahead and kill yourselves! See if I care!"

And she turned away and ran down the corridor.

Larry was too thunderstruck to go after her. Besides, he knew she was right.

Chapter 10

The conference room filled slowly with Council members. At the head of the table, standing there and watching them drift in, Larry thought they looked almost reluctant to get the meeting started.

They know that a battle's coming; they've got a hard choice to make, and they don't want to face it.

His own thoughts kept slipping back to Valery, to the angry, sad, scared look in her eyes the night before. *She can't stay away from us both,* he knew. The ship's laws were lenient in some ways, but inexorable in others. Valery was at the age for marriage. She must marry. The computer's genetics program had listed the men who were genetically suited for marriage with her. There was no way for her to avoid it; she had to marry someone on that list.

Either Dan or me, Larry thought. Then, *Or somebody else? No, she couldn't marry somebody else. She wouldn't.*

But now there was another part to the problem. *If the Council decides to stay at Alpha Centauri, then we'll have to genetically alter this next generation of children. Val's children—whoever she marries—will be sulfur-breathing, high-gravity monsters. She won't be able to*

*live with them; they couldn't stay in the same sections of
the ship, except for brief visits. They couldn't breathe the
same air.*

Someone coughed, and Larry snapped his attention
back to the conference room, the Council meeting, the
men and women who were now in their seats and looking
up at him.

Only three seats were still vacant: Dr. Loring's, Joe
Haller's, and Dan's. Before Larry could say anything, the
door at the far end of the room slid open and Haller and
Dan stepped in. Dan was smiling.

They took their seats at that end of the table, and
Larry sat in his chair.

"I assume you've all reviewed the minutes of our last
meeting, and know the agenda for today."

A general mumble and nodding of heads.

"We've all seen Dr. Polanyi's data tapes from the
probes."

Assent again.

The nervousness that Larry had expected to feel just
wasn't there. He hunched forward in his chair, feeling
. . . detached, remote from all this, as if he himself, the
real Larry Belsen was somewhere lightyears away, looking back and watching the meeting, watching the person
in his skin the way a scientist watches an experimental
animal.

Leaning his forearms on the table, Larry said, "All
right, we can get right down to it. The basic question is
simply this: do we end our voyage at Alpha Centauri, or
do we go on to try to find a better, more Earthlike planet
at another star?"

For a moment none of the Council members said anything; they looked at each other, none of them apparently willing to start the debate.

Then Mort Campbell cleared his throat. His voice was deep, his usual speech pattern was slow and methodical. Put together with his solid frame and beefy face, he gave the impression of being a stolid, slow muscleman. But Campbell was the ship's champion chess player, as well as its top wrestler. His scientific skills, as chief of the Life Support group, spanned medicine, cryogenics, electronics, and most of the engineering disciplines. When he talked, no matter how slowly, people listened.

"I can't really say much about the choice we have," he rumbled. "But I do know something about the life support equipment on board this ship. We're in no condition to go farther. The air regenerators, the waste cyclers, the cryonics units, the rest of it—everything's being held together with that leftover gunk from the cafeteria that the cooks call coffee, plus what little hair I have left."

Several people chuckled. Campbell grinned lazily.

"Seriously," he continued, "I think it's foolish to talk about going farther." He turned toward Dan's end of the table. "How about you lads in Propulsion and Power? Is your equipment in as bad a shape as mine?"

Dan gestured with one hand. "We haven't started pulling out our hair yet, but the reactors and generators aren't going to last another five-six decades. Not even five or six more years."

"And what choice do we have?" Joe Haller asked. "There's no evidence of a better planet anywhere."

"Dr. Loring was searching for such evidence when his accident occurred," Dr. Polanyi said. "Unfortunately, there was no record of his work in the computer memory core."

Larry started to reply, but Polanyi went on, "However, I received a call last night from Dr. Loring's daughter. She believes she has found some of her father's handwritten notes, and she would like to tell the Council about them."

"What?" *Val's got evidence of her father's work?*

Suddenly Larry was totally alert, every nerve tight, every muscle tense.

He forced his voice to stay calm as he asked, "What do you mean, Dr. Polanyi?"

The old engineer shrugged. "Exactly what I said. Miss Loring apparently has uncovered some of her father's notes, and she feels she can tell us something, at least, about the progress of his work."

Larry glanced down the table at Dan. He seemed just as surprised as Larry himself felt.

"Then we ought to hear what she has to tell us," Larry said.

Nodding vigorously, Polanyi answered, "Precisely. I took the liberty of asking her to wait in the outer room. Shall I call her in?"

Larry looked around the table. No dissenting voices. "Yes," he said. "Ask her to come in."

Polanyi got up from his seat and went to the door nearest Larry's end of the table. He slid it open and gestured; Valery stepped into the conference room. She was wearing a dress instead of her usual slacks or coveralls; she looked very serious. And tired.

She must have stayed up all night.

"Why don't you take your father's seat," Larry suggested to her.

She nodded to him and went to the empty chair. Polanyi held it for her.

Dan called, "You have some evidence about your father's attempts to find other Earthlike planets?"

Valery's voice was low, weary. "Well, I don't know if you can call it evidence, exactly. It's just some scribbled notes that he left in our quarters, in his desk. I found them accidentally last night. . . . I was going to write a letter. . . ." She glanced up at Larry, then turned and looked straight across the table at Polanyi.

"The notes don't make much sense by themselves, but they reminded me of some of the conversations we had at home. . . . Father liked to talk about his work, you know."

She hesitated a moment. Larry could see that she was fighting to keep her self-control, struggling to keep her mind away from her father's accident—and who caused it.

"He was trying to determine what kinds of planets are associated with two particular stars: Epsilon Indi and Epsilon Eridani. Both are orange, K-sequence stars, somewhat cooler than the sun. Both definitely have planets orbiting around them. That much he was sure of."

"There are lots of other stars that are just as close as those two, or closer, aren't there?" Adrienne Kaufman asked.

Valery nodded. "Yes, but they're almost all red dwarf-stars—so dim and cool that the chance for finding a planet with Earthlike temperatures, liquid water, and livable conditions—well, the chances are almost nil."

"I see."

Someone asked, "These planets your father was studying, are they like Earth?"

"That's what he was trying to determine," Val answered, "when . . . when he was injured."

Larry could feel the electric tension around the table.

"As nearly as I could make out from his notes, and from the few conversations we had on the subject," Val went on, "he had determined that Epsilon Indi—the nearer of the two stars—had more than one planet. Its major planet is a gas giant, like Jupiter, completely unfit for us."

"And the others?"

She shook her head. "He never found out. He had been talking about building better electronic boosters for the main telescope. I guess he needed better magnification and resolution to study the smaller planets."

"We could build such equipment," Dr. Polanyi said. "But who would use it? Dr. Loring was our only qualified astronomer."

"Perhaps we could revive an astronomer who's now in cryosleep."

"Are there any?"

Valery raised her voice a notch. "If the Council will allow it, I would like to handle the astronomical work myself."

"You?"

"I realize that my place is in Computing. But I've always followed my father's work very closely, and I think that I'm the best qualified person here for continuing his studies. . . . Unless, of course, you want to go to the trouble to revive a sleeping astronomer."

"But can you make the necessary observations in less than a month? Otherwise we must go into orbit around the Centaurian planet."

"I haven't the faintest idea," Valery replied.

"We're going to have to take up a parking orbit around the planet anyway," Dan said firmly.

Everyone turned to him.

"I've been checking with all the different groups on board. Mr. Campbell's little speech earlier was the last stroke. Just about every group says their equipment needs to be overhauled, repaired, rebuilt. . . . We can't keep expecting the ship to function indefinitely without major repairs."

He pushed his chair back and stood up. "We can't make major repairs while we're running all the equipment full blast. But if we go into orbit around the planet, we can afford to shut down some sections of the ship for weeks or even months at a time."

"And once we're in orbit around the planet," Larry countered, "the temptation to stay and make it our new home might just become overpowering. Right?"

Dan shrugged. "Could be. All I know is that the reactors need deuterium. Our supplies are too low to last much longer—a few years, at most. That planet has water on it, so there must be deuterium there, too. It's that simple."

"So we must stop. Whether we want to or not," Larry said.

Dan nodded, smiling.

Everyone else around the table was nodding, too. Larry saw that there was nothing he could do about it. He was outmaneuvered, outvoted, outsmarted. The whole business of trying to decide what to do was a complete shambles. They were going to fall into orbit around the Centaurian planet, no matter what.

"I believe," Dr. Polanyi said, "that orbiting the planet may have some definite advantages. We will be able to study it close-up, even go down onto the surface with exploration teams. Miss Loring can use the time to make further astronomical observations. And we can repair and refurbish the ship at our leisure. After all, even if we decide to stay at Alpha Centauri, those of us who are alive now will still have to spend the rest of their existence aboard ship. We will not be able to live on the surface."

Dan said, "But our children will."

Val's children, Larry thought bitterly.

"All right," he said aloud. "It seems there's no way around it, and therefore we don't need to decide about heading elsewhere. Not right now, at least." He turned to the chief medic. "Will you please start the procedure for reviving an astronaut team? It looks like we're going to be sending groups of people down to the planet's surface."

The meditech nodded.

The meeting broke up soon afterward. As people got up from their seats and headed for the doors, Larry went straight to Val.

"You didn't tell me about your father's notes," he said.

She was standing by the table, looking very serious and even more beautiful than he had ever known before.

"It happened just as I said." Her voice was strained, as if she was trying to keep any emotion out of it. "I went to the desk to write a letter to Dan, to tell him what I'd told you, and found father's handwritten notes in the drawer."

"You haven't changed your mind . . . about last night."

She looked away from him. "No. I'm not going to be the reason for you and Dan to hurt each other. I simply refuse."

"But what's this about you doing astronomical work? I didn't know . . ."

"There are lots of things about me that you don't know," Val said. "But I know all about you and Dan. Both of you think the other one deliberately tried to kill Father. Well, if someone else started to work in the observatory, what's to stop the would-be killer—if there is one—from attacking him?"

Realization dawned on Larry, together with a sinking feeling in the pit of his stomach. "You mean that if you're the one working in the observatory . . ."

"Neither you nor Dan will hurt me. There. It sounds silly and terrible at the same time, doesn't it? But if you're both convinced that one of you is a murderer, then the only person who *can* continue the astronomical work has to be me."

"But . . . suppose there is a murderer, and it's neither one of us? Suppose it's somebody else?"

Valery didn't hesitate an instant. "If that happens, then

maybe you two idiots can work together to find out who the real madman is!"

She turned and headed for the door. From the set of her slim shoulders, the stubborn toss of her golden hair, Larry could see quite clearly that she didn't want him to try walking with her.

He sagged back against the table, feeling utterly drained. *The whole world is falling apart . . . everything's breaking up and there's nothing I can do. . . .*

Then a thought struck him. Dan had said that they'd have to get fresh deuterium for the reactors from the water on the planet. That meant sending a complex load of equipment down to the surface, together with people trained to run it. *It means Dan will have to go down to the surface of the planet.* The dangerous, maybe deadly surface.

Larry almost smiled.

Chapter 11

Guido Estelella was an astronaut, the only man on ship—asleep or awake—who had experience in piloting rocket craft from orbit down to the surface of a planet and back up again. He hadn't been one of the political prisoners, back when the ship had been an orbital jail, a place of exile for Earth's scientists. He had been a free man, an astronaut by training. It was his joy.

But the same Earth government that made prisoners of thousands of scientists and sent them into orbital exile with their families had also cut space flight down to almost nothing. Orbital flights, mostly to repair communications and weather satellites; a few flights to the Moon each year, bringing workers to the factories there. That was all. No more Mars flights. No further exploration of the solar system. Earth could not afford it.

So when the prisoners coaxed Earth's government into letting them drive their orbiting prison out toward the stars, Estelella volunteered to join them.

"After all," said he, "it's my namesake, isn't it?"

So he went to the stars, frozen in cryosleep for nearly fifty years, to be awakened when he was needed. Now he was awake and working.

And most unhappy.

Guido Estelella stood in an insulated pressure suit on the surface of the new world. Everyone else called it Major, a contraction from "Alpha Centauri's major planet." But in his own mind, Estelella called it Femina: a woman, a certain kind of woman—beautiful, selfish, treacherous, hot-tempered, dangerous.

He always felt tired here. Maybe it was the high gravity, putting an extra load on his muscles. Maybe it was just the constant fear.

For six weeks now, Guido had been flying a small landing craft down to the ground from the main ship, which was now orbiting five hundred kilometers above the planet's equator. At least twice each week he carried men and equipment down to the small base camp they had made by the shore of one of Femina's landlocked seas. The rest of the time he trained youngsters to fly the landing craft. There had been one wreck, killing two men and a girl. There had been several very close calls. Guido had aged more in the past six weeks than he did in his fifty years of cryosleep. Far more.

At the moment he was standing halfway between the stubby, winged landing rocket and the sprawl of equipment and plastic bubble tents that made up the base camp. A strong wind was whipping the green water of the sea into whitecaps, but inside his pressure suit, Guido felt the wind only as a faint screeching sound, muffled by his earphones. What was bothering him wasn't the wind, but the ugly brownish-yellow cloud that it was carrying toward them from the sea horizon.

"Ship to camp," a girl's voice crackled in his earphones. "We've confirmed that there's a new volcano active on the far coast of your sea, and the prevailing wind is bringing the fallout in your direction."

Guido nodded unhappily inside his helmet. He clicked a button on his waistband panel.

"I think we'd better get the shuttle up and out of here before that cloud arrives."

"Take off early? But we're not ready." It was Dan Christopher's voice, coming from the camp, much stronger than the ship's transmission.

Guido began to head toward the shuttle craft. "The last time I saw a cloud like that, it brought with it a lightning storm that kept us grounded for two days. And the rain had such a high sulfur content and so many stones in it that we had to resurface the entire top of the shuttle. The heat shield, even the pilot's bubble were pitted and etched. I don't want to get caught on the ground like that again."

"But you can't take all of us with you. Some of us will have to stay here during the storm. And the equipment . . ."

"My first responsibility is for the shuttle. Your equipment is protected, and you can sit out the storm in the underground shelter." He reached the shuttle's hatch, popped open the access panel, and pressed the stud inside. The hatch cracked open and the ladder unfolded at his feet.

"Wait," Dan's voice responded. "I'll send out as many people as we can. How many do you have room for?"

"Four. Unless you want to remove some of the cargo we packed aboard this morning."

"The deuterium? No chance. It's worth a helluva lot more than any of us."

Guido looked at the sea. It was frothing heavily now, steep breakers building up and dumping their energy on the sandy shore. The grass and trees were swaying in the mounting wind. The cloud was closer, spreading, blotting out the sunshine and the golden sky.

"I can wait about ten minutes," he said.

Inside the main bubble tent of the camp, Dan frowned and glared at the radio set. The main tent was a hodge-podge of radio equipment, viewscreens, cooking units, tables, crated supplies, folding tables and chairs, and five busy people.

Dan could hear the wind's growing anger outside. One of the girls seated at an analysis workbench glanced up at the roof of their transparent bubble: the plastic was rippling in the wind, making an odd kind of crinkling noise that they'd never heard before. It had taken them days to get accustomed to things like wind, and the noises that an open world makes. Now it was starting to sound frightening.

"Nancy, Tania, Vic . . . you three get into suits right away and get to the ship. Ross, you and I are going to stay. Vic, bring the latest tank of deuterium with you."

"But it's less than half full," Vic argued.

Dan waved him down. "I know, but we'd better get it shipboard. No telling how bad this storm can get; might damage the equipment. The deuterium's far too valuable to risk."

Vic nodded.

"Get into a suit," Dan said. "Ross and I will hang on here."

Ross Cranston glanced sharply at Dan, but said nothing. He didn't like being second-best to a meter-tall tank of stainless steel, even though he knew that the deuterium gas inside it *was* more important to the ship than any computer operator.

The two girls and Vic were suited up in a few minutes, moving slowly in the heavy gravity. Vic hefted the tank by its handles, his knees giving slightly under its weight.

"Can you manage it?" Dan asked anxiously.

"Yeah." Vic's voice was muffled by his helmet.

The three of them cycled through the airlock and started trudging heavily through the wind-blown sand and grit toward the sleek little shuttle rocket. Dan watched them through the tent's transparent plastic. The two girls each grabbed a handle of the tank and helped Vic to carry it.

Turning, Dan saw that Ross was already at the hatch to the underground shelter.

"I'm going to suit up and make a last check of the refining equipment," Dan told him. He had to raise his voice to make himself heard over the wind, even though Ross was only a few meters away.

Ross nodded, visibly unhappy.

"Stay by the radio while I'm outside," Dan said as he reached for one of the two remaining pressure suits hanging stiffly by the airlock.

Ross frowned, but nodded again.

He's scared, Dan said to himself. *Scared of the storm, and scared that I might get hurt and need him to come out and help me.*

Neither of them had been on the ground when the first storm had struck, several weeks ago. Two people had been badly hurt when the wind toppled their communications antenna squarely onto the main tent. After that, the underground shelter was dug and the antenna was moved away from the rest of the camp.

By the time Dan had his suit zipped up, the shuttle's rocket engines had roared to life, out-howling even the mounting fury of the storm. Dan reached for his helmet and held it in both hands as he watched the shuttle trundle forward on its landing wheels, then gather speed and scream past the tent toward the beach. Its image shimmered and grew hazy in the heat from its own exhaust, but, squinting, Dan made out the delta-shaped craft as its nose lifted from the ground. It rolled along on its rear wheels for a moment longer, then it seemed to shoot almost straight upward, angling into the sky like a white arrowhead against the gathering darkness of the clouds.

In less than a minute the rolling thunder of the rocket's takeoff had rumbled away, leaving only the keening of the wind and the flapping of the tent's supposedly tearproof plastic.

As he put the helmet on, Dan thought, *There's a big difference between seeing storms on videotapes and really being in one.*

He checked the suit radio. "I'm going out now, Ross."

"Okay."

Dan turned to see Ross through the helmet's faceplate. The computerman looked scared and sullen.

"If you go down into the shelter, tell me before you leave the radio. I don't want to be stuck alone out there."

"I will."

Dan nodded and opened the inner airlock hatch. While

the airlock was busy sealing itself and pumping out the good breathable air, Dan was trying to calm himself.

He wasn't frightened, he was excited; happy, really. He knew that was dangerous. *If you're scared, like Ross, you don't take chances.* But Dan was soaring high, spaced out on the excitement of being on the surface of a planet, *the* planet, the new world, facing its dangers unafraid. The storm, the wind, the crashing of the sea, the tossing golden trees, the dust and sand that was blowing through the air in ever-thickening clouds—it was wild and free. Not like the ship. Not like the quiet, orderly world where everything went according to schedule and there was absolutely no difference between one day and the next. This was *life!*

The airlock lights turned green. Dan clumped heavily to the outer hatch and turned its control wheel. It moved slowly, slowly, then the hatch popped open and a gust of grit-filled air puffed into the airlock.

Dan had to lean hard against the hatch to get it to swing open wide enough for him to go outside. Already his muscles felt strained. The high gravity made everything feel heavier than it should: the suit weighed down on him, the hatch opened grudgingly. It was an effort to lift one booted foot off the floor of the airlock and place it on the sandy soil outside.

The wind caught Dan by surprise. He had heard it long enough, but now he felt it as physical force. Even inside the suit he could feel the wind buffeting him, trying to push him down.

He grinned.

Turning his back to the wind, he began trudging along

the edge of the circular tent, heading for the once-gleaming jumble of metal shapes that was the refinery.

It gleamed no longer. Many weeks of being exposed to this corrosive atmosphere had dulled its exterior finish, and the storms and rains had etched and pitted the metal. *But the insides still work,* Dan told himself as he looked along the length of pipes that led down to the sea. Take in sea water, extract the deuterium, then return what's left—about 99.97 percent of it. *We don't want much from you,* Dan said silently to the sea. *Just three hundredths of a percent. Enough to live on.*

A shriek of metal against metal made him jump in sudden fear. From inside the helmet, he couldn't see what was happening. He had to turn around and lean his whole body backward to look up.

One of the solar battery panels—the collection of silicon-based cells that converted sunlight into electricity—had ripped loose from the roof of the refinery's storage tower. Now it was sliding along the bulbous metal domes of the separation equipment, banging, screeching . . . It blew free and sailed like a jagged enormous leaf into the wind, pinwheeling as it disappeared into the dust clouds that were blowing everywhere.

"Never worked right anyway!" Dan yelled. The solar batteries had been badly eroded by the sulfur-rich air. Dan had been forced to fly a small generator down from the ship to provide electricity for the base camp.

Everything else on this side of the equipment complex looked tight and safe. *Even if the other solar panels rip off, that's no problem. Unless they tear into the tent.*

Dan's legs were starting to tremble with exertion. He

forced himself to plod around the side of the big refinery. As he turned the corner, the wind caught him head-on and nearly toppled him backward. Leaning heavily into the wind, he trudged on.

It was getting very dark now. And the wind was screaming insanely. Dust clouds made it hard to see any distance at all.

Lightning flashed. Dan heard it crackle in his earphones as it flickered out over the sea, brightening the whole scene for an eyeblink's time. It sent a jolt of irrational fear through him.

Then came the boom of the thunder, distant but menacing. Dan moved on.

He couldn't see the radio antenna in the darkness and dust. Then another flash of lightning and there it was, swaying like a gigantic, leafless, branchless tree. But it held firm. The new anchor pins were doing their job.

A sudden gust of wind actually lifted one of Dan's boots off the ground. He swayed for a moment, fought hard for balance, then planted the foot back on the ground.

"Ross?" he called into his helmet microphone.

No answer.

"Ross! Are you there? I'm coming in . . . be back in a minute."

Silence. Only the crackling of lightning static in his earphones. *He's gone back into the shelter*, Dan realized.

Bending into the wind, Dan clumped forward slowly. It was painful, each step. Another horrible tearing sound, and he saw out of the corner of his eye another of the solar panels flipping off madly, hitting the ground with one corner and bouncing along like a child's runaway toy.

Then a more ominous sound. A groaning, gut-wrenching sound, like the earth itself being pulled apart. Dan looked up at the metal domes and towers alongside him, but couldn't see any cause for the . . .

It moaned again. And fainter, the sound of—flapping. Something soft, something plastic . . . *the tent!*

Dan pushed himself madly along the side of the refinery, trying to get to the side where the tent stood. If it still stood. He stumbled and fell face forward, but hardly stopped at all. He crawled on all fours for a few paces, then painfully pushed himself to his feet again. The wind was getting intolerable.

Grabbing hold of a projecting ladder-rung from the metal tower he stood next to, swaying in the howling insanity of the wind, Dan rested for a moment, then pushed on. He rounded the corner and saw what the groaning noise was.

The tent was collapsed and flapping on the ground like some monstrous dying pterodactyl. Dan couldn't see the airlock, couldn't tell if Ross had made it to the underground shelter before the collapse. If he hadn't, he was dead inside there.

Only one thing was certain. There was no way for Dan to get inside to safety.

The storm howled triumphantly.

In the ship's observation center, at the zero-gravity hub, the only sound was the faintest whispering of the air-circulating fans.

Larry hovered weightlessly at the transparent wall of

the big plastiglass blister, staring out at the massive curving bulk of the golden planet below. A huge yellow-brown smear was staining one section of the planet's surface: the storm.

He touched the plastiglass wall with his fingertips, anchoring himself lightly in place. There was a wall phone within arm's reach, but he didn't want to use it, didn't want to hear what was happening.

"Dan's still down there."

Before he turned, he knew it was Valery's voice. In the golden light coming up from the planet, she looked like an ancient goddess, shining against the darkness of the observation center's dim lighting. Her face, though, was very human: worried, almost frightened.

Larry said, "The shuttle came back about fifteen minutes ago. Estelella brought the two girls and Vic O'Malley with him. Dan and Cranston stayed. Dan made certain that he sent every gram of deuterium they had processed."

"And now he's in the middle of the storm." Her voice was calm, but just barely. Larry could hear the beginnings of a tremble in it.

"They've got the underground shelter. He'll be all right."

"Has he sent word? Do you know for sure . . . ?"

Larry jerked a thumb toward the storm cloud. "Can't get radio transmission through that stuff. We've tried every frequency. Too much electrical interference."

"He could be dead."

"No. He's tough and smart. He'll get through it all right."

She stared out at the swirling muddy-colored storm cloud. "It looks alive . . . like some monster eating. . . ." Val reached out for Larry. "Can't you do *anything*? Send the shuttle down for him? Something!"

He took her in his arms and rocked her gently. "There's not a thing we can do but wait. The shuttle would be wrecked trying to fly through that. All we can do is wait." And his mind was asking him, *If it were you down there and Dan safely up here, would she be this upset?*

"It makes you feel so helpless," Val whimpered.

"I know. I know."

"How long will the storm last?"

Larry shrugged. "Nobody knows. Not enough data on the weather patterns of this planet. The last one took two days to blow past the camp. But we don't know it if was an unusually big one, or . . ." He let his voice trail off.

"Or an unusually small one," Valery finished for him. "This one looks bigger, doesn't it?"

Larry didn't answer.

She kept staring out at the planet, at the storm. "Oh, Larry, if he dies there . . ."

"It'll be my fault."

Val turned sharply enough to bounce slightly away from the plastiglass. "Your fault? Why should it be your fault?"

"I sent him down there, didn't I?"

"It's part of his job. He wanted to go."

Larry said, "I could have stopped him. I could have ordered somebody else to go down instead. I knew it was dangerous down there."

Val was drifting freely in a small semicircle around

Larry. He had to turn his back to the plastiglass to keep his eyes on her. She floated in midair, a golden goddess shining against the night.

"Did you *want* him to be exposed to danger?" she asked.

"You mean, did I want him to risk getting killed?" Larry closed his eyes and found the answer in his mind. "No, I didn't."

"Not consciously," Val murmured.

"What?"

"You knew he'd be running into danger."

Nodding, Larry admitted, "Sure. I even thought about going down there with him . . . but I'm not qualified for any of the jobs that need doing down there. I couldn't justify taking up space on the shuttle and in the camp, just to show everybody I'm as brave as Dan is."

"But in the back of your mind you knew he might be killed."

"Of course. But that doesn't mean . . ." He began to see what she was driving at. "Val, you don't think that I . . . you *can't* believe that!"

"I don't," she said. But it sounded weak, unconvincing.

Larry thought, *It would certainly settle all the problems if he got killed down there.* Then another part of his mind screamed, *And that would make you a murderer, whether you planned it beforehand or not!*

Valery seemed to sense the turmoil in his mind. She took him by the hand and pushed against the plastiglass wall, driving the two of them into a slow drift across the big, darkened, empty-looking chamber.

"I guess you're right," she said over her shoulder to

him. "There's not much we can do except watch and wait."

"Val . . . I didn't want it this way, honestly. I didn't . . ."

"I know," she said soothingly. "I know."

They touched down on the floor easily, their velcroed slippers catching and holding gently against the carpeting there.

"As long as we're here," Valery said, letting his hand go and walking carefully, in a slow zero-g glide, toward the desk and instruments in the middle of the room, "I might as well show you what I've found out about the other stars."

She's changing the subject, Larry realized, *trying to get both our minds off Dan.*

Val sat at the desk while Larry stood beside her. She touched buttons on the desktop keyboard and pictures appeared on the viewscreen.

To Larry, they all looked like tiny white dots. The stars were bigger and brighter; in some pictures they were glaringly bright. But the planets around the stars were all featureless blobs of light.

Valery shook her head after showing about twenty of the pictures. "Those are the best we have so far. And it's all pretty depressing. Nothing even close to being Earth-like."

Larry blinked at her. "None of those planets . . ."

"They're mostly gas giants, like Jupiter. Or little balls of rock, like Earth's Moon."

"Can you be sure?"

She ran a hand through her hair. "Oh, I'm still working

on it, trying to get better data, more precision in the spectrograms and visuals . . . but it looks very bad."

Larry sagged into a half-sitting, half-leaning position against the desk's edge. "And this goes for both Epsilon Indi and Epsilon Eridani."

"Yes, both stars. I'm afraid the planet here is the only choice we're going to have, Larry."

He sat there a moment longer, his mind turning slowly, wearily. "When . . . when will you report this to the Council?"

"I want to make the data much more precise," she answered. "I haven't shown this to anyone yet . . . you're the only one. In a week or two, I'll report it to the Council."

He nodded dumbly.

Valery went to turn off the last picture from the viewscreen. "Oops!" She pulled her hand away from the keyboard as if it were burning hot. "I almost hit the ERASE button. That would've been stupid."

"Huh?"

"All this data—weeks and weeks of work—would be erased from the computer's memory bank if I had touched that button just now." She pressed the proper button and the viewscreen went blank. Looking up at Larry, she added, "The only two places where the data's stored are in the computer's memory bank . . . and my own head."

Larry nodded at her, but said nothing.

Chapter 12

The wind was getting even worse.

Dan tried to flatten himself into a niche between two of the big water-treatment tanks, but he felt the wind tearing at him, trying to pry him loose and bowl him along like the solar panels had been blown away. It was getting hard to stay on his feet. The noise was overpowering, and he could barely see a dozen meters ahead because of the dust and flying sand. He could hear the gritty stuff grinding against his suit; a yellowish film was building up on his helmet faceplate. He wiped at it awkwardly with a gloved hand, smearing it even worse than before.

Can't stay here, he knew. *Got to get into the shelter.*

He edged away from the metal tanks far enough to poke his head around their curving flanks and look at the tent. A sudden gust of wind nearly knocked him over. The tent was flapping wildly in the roaring wind, snapping and tearing like a huge blanket. It cracked against one of the slim metal pipes leading from the squat round dome of the centrifuge and the pipe went *clang!* and snapped in half. Dan suddenly got a picture of what would happen if that tent-whip hit him.

It was getting difficult to move the arms of his suit.

Muscles tired . . . or are the joints getting jammed with grit? Probably both.

Then he started wondering what would happen if his suit sprung a leak, if the sulfurous air ate through his plastic oxygen tubing, if the grit made the suit completely immovable, if . . .

Stop it! he commanded himself. *Try to think. Think calmly. Are you safer here or should you try to get into the shelter?*

The question was answered for him. A half-dozen spears of lightning flickered off in the distance, far enough to be still out over the sea, close enough so that the thunder exploded almost immediately with shattering noise.

Lightning! Dan remembered what he'd been told about the last storm. The lightning bolts loved the big high-standing metal equipment that stood there. Dozens of bolts had hit the refinery.

If I'm out here when the lightning starts striking . . .

He knew he had to get to the shelter.

Slowly, carefully, Dan hunkered down onto his knees and then flattened out on his belly. The wind-blown dust was even worse down at ground level; he could barely see an arm's length before him. The wind tried to lift him up off the ground, sail him like a glider. He pressed himself into the ground as hard as he could.

He crawled. Centimeter by agonized centimeter, he crawled on all fours toward the tent. He was guided more by the flapping, whip-cracking sounds of the tent's loose fabric than by vision. All he could see was flying sand and wind-flattened yellow grass.

It seemed to take hours. Dan knew it was only a few meters from where he had been standing to the edge of the tent, but it seemed more like lightyears now. A new blast of lightning turned everything glare-white for an instant, and the thunder seemed to be trying to crack him open like an eggshell. Every muscle in his body ached and burned, and he was drenched with sweat.

Got to stop . . . rest . . . But something inside him said fiercely, *Stop now and you're dead. Keep going, dammit! Keep going!*

He inched along. A lightning bolt struck metal somewhere close beside him with an unbelievable burst of light and a deafening explosion. Something hit Dan's right leg and the suit seemed to go completely stiff there. He couldn't move the leg at all.

Or is my own leg hurt? He didn't feel any extra pain there, but he knew that shock sometimes cut off pain. And besides, every part of him already hurt so much. . . .

His outstretched hand bumped into something. The flat, circular plastisteel foundation of the tent.

Dan raised his head and saw the tent's fabric looming up, flapping wildly, right in front of him. Like a nightmare monster. Rising up, up, filling all his vision with its rippling, snapping immensity. Then with a whip-crack it flattened out again, only to begin rising once more immediately.

Can't go through that, Dan realized.

He fumbled at his belt for the suit's tool kit. It was almost impossible to feel shapes with the gloves on, but at last he pulled out the little pistol-shaped laser that they used for cutting and welding.

Hope it's charged up. Dan pressed the snub nose of the laser against the edge of the tent's foundation and pulled on the trigger. The pistol didn't make a sound or vibration, but after a moment or two Dan could see the plastic fabric of the tent glowing, tearing, separating from the foundation.

With an agonized screeching sound, the plastic ripped free of the foundation and went billowing into the wind, disappearing into the howling storm like a giant bird suddenly let loose.

Dan clung to the foundation's edge for a long, weary moment, then pulled himself slowly over the lip. He dragged himself, using his arms and his one movable leg, groping for the hatch to the underground shelter. Desks, chairs, viewscreens, even the heavy computer consoles had been blown over by the wind, bowled away like so much dust. Another bolt of lightning struck with shattering force, blinding and deafening Dan for several moments.

Then his hands found the hatch. He pulled himself up onto his elbows, nearly unconscious with pain and exhaustion. Eyes stinging and nearly blinded with sweat, he groped for the control switch. He found it and leaned on it heavily. It wouldn't move. He forced his weight on the tiny switch as hard as he could. Nothing.

Jammed by the grit.

He raised a fist, taking all the strength he had, and pounded on the hatch itself. *If Cranston's down there . . . if he's not dead . . .* Even his thoughts were getting fuzzy now. Pound. Raise the fist and let it drop. Raise the . . . fist and . . . let it *drop*.

The hatch moved! It pushed against his inert arm. A straining, rasping sound and Dan could see the hatch lifting slowly. A gloved hand was pushing it open from the inside.

Everything seemed to go hazy, foggy, blood-red and then dead-black. Dan could feel his body moving—being moved?—and the noise of the wind's evil howling dimmed, muffled. Somebody was talking to him, urgent words crackling in his earphones. Then the blackness swam up and surrounded him and pulled him downward into oblivion.

When he awoke, his helmet was off. Cranston was completely out of his suit, dressed only in blue coveralls. The little underground shelter seemed cool and snug and safe. The wind was a distant mumble somewhere outside. The shelter was bright and quiet. Its curving walls and ceiling seemed to gather around him protectively. Its bunk felt soft and comfortable.

Cranston was standing by the cooking unit.

"Do you think you could eat something?" he asked, looking worriedly at Dan.

Dan realized he was sitting on one of the bunks, slouched against the curving wall of the shelter.

"Yeh . . . sure." Every muscle ached. His head throbbed horribly. His mouth felt dry and caked with dust.

Glancing down at his legs, he saw that Cranston had taken off the bottom half of his suit, as well as his helmet.

"There was a bad dent on the left leg of the suit," the computerman said. "I was worried that your own leg might've been hurt. It's bruised pretty bad, but I don't think it's anything worse than that."

"When . . ." Dan tried to lick his lips, but his tongue was dry. He croaked, "When did you . . . come into the shelter?"

Cranston flashed him a guilty glance, then turned his attention to the cooker. "Uh . . . I tried calling you on the radio . . . no answer. I didn't know what was happening. Then . . . uh, the tent . . . it looked like it was going to collapse. . . ."

"It did," Dan said wearily. "You did the best thing."

"Oh . . . okay . . ." He smiled, still looking slightly guilty.

Dr. Hsai's quarters looked like pictures of Japanese homes that Valery had seen on the education tapes.

The compartment was no bigger than any other single man's quarters. But it looked different. There were living green vines climbing along one wall, reaching upward to the ceiling light panels. A painting filled part of the same wall, showing soft green hills and a river with a delicate bridge arching over it. The vines seemed to blend into the picture, the two merged and became a single experience. The bunk was austere, hard-looking, but a beautiful red drape hung beside it. There was no other furniture visible, except two little pillows on the floor and a low-slung black lacquered table.

Dr. Hsai himself was dressed in a loose-fitting robe of black and white, with just a hint of gold thread at the collar.

"What a beautiful robe!" Valery said, despite herself, as Dr. Hsai ushered her into his quarters.

"Thank you very much." The psychotech smiled pleasantly. "It belonged to my great-grandfather and has been handed down through four generations."

"It's very lovely."

He smiled again and bowed ever so slightly. "I am afraid," he said, "that I have no western furniture for you to sit upon. I usually receive visitors in the office of the infirmary. But you seemed so insistent. . . ."

"I can sit on the floor," Val said. She curled up next to the bunk.

Dr. Hsai offered her one of the pillows, and Val put it behind the small of her back, then leaned against the edge of the bunk.

"You wish to ask me a medical question?" Dr. Hsai inquired, sitting in the middle of the tiny room.

"A psychological question," Val replied.

He nodded. "I might have guessed. Unfortunately, my knowledge of psychiatry is far from expert, although I have been studying the available tapes on the subject very carefully these past few weeks."

"Why?" Val asked. "Do you think there's a killer aboard the ship, too?"

Hsai smiled patiently. "Not at all. At least, I hope not. But certain individuals believe that there might be a killer among us, and I am trying to pin down the origins of these fears."

"There have been these . . . accidents."

"Yes."

"Including my father."

"Yes."

Valery was starting to feel uncomfortable. What she wanted to ask suddenly began to sound silly in her own mind. Worse still, she felt that Dr. Hsai knew what she wanted, but was being too polite to bring up the subject himself.

"Dan Christopher has been under great emotional stress," the psychotech said, mainly to keep the conversation from faltering. "He is a very troubled young man. Perhaps it would have been wise to revive one or more of our sleeping psychiatrists, to examine him thoroughly."

"Yes, I was wondering why you didn't do that," Val said.

"Larry Belsen said it wouldn't be necessary. As Chairman, he has the responsibility to pass on all requests for revival."

"Larry disapproved?"

"Yes. I asked him specifically if he wanted us to revive a psychiatrist. . . . It was when Dan Christopher was in the infirmary for observation, and I could find nothing psychologically wrong with him."

"And Larry said he didn't want a psychiatrist revived?"

Dr. Hsai almost frowned. "Not in those words, but he told me he thought it would be unnecessary. You know, of course, the difficulties involved in reviving a person, and the limited resources we have. It cannot be done lightly. And we cannot ask the person, once revived, to return to sleep a few days or weeks later. It is not medically wise, for one thing."

"I know." Valery suddenly realized that she was gnawing on her lip. A nervous habit. She looked back at Dr. Hsai. "About the question I wanted to ask you . . ."

"So?"

Somehow it didn't feel so silly now. "Could . . . could a person do things—violent things—and not know it?"

Hsai looked puzzled.

"I mean, could somebody commit a murder and then not remember he did it? You know, his conscious mind doesn't even know what he's really doing."

Hsai gave the faintest of shrugs. "I have heard of such cases in my education, of course, but . . . of course, I have never dealt with such a situation myself."

Before she could think about it, Valery spilled out, "Do you think that the reason Larry didn't want a psychiatrist revived is that he was afraid the psychiatrist might find out something about him—about Larry himself?"

For an instant, Hsai looked shocked. Then he dropped a mask of oriental and professional calm over his face. "You believe that Larry Belsen might be unbalanced?"

"My father's injury was no accident," Val said, feeling miserable. "Somebody did it. Either Dan or Larry . . . or somebody else."

For several moments Dr. Hsai sat there silently, his eyes closed. Then he looked up and said, "I will immediately take steps to revive the ship's best psychiatrists. If your suspicions are even remotely close to the truth, this is an emergency situation. There is no need to wait for the Chairman's approval under these circumstances."

"The only trouble is," Val said, "that Dan might already be dead."

Chapter 13

Dan knew it was a nightmare, yet it still had him terrified.

He was running, or trying to. He seemed to be caught in some thick syrupy liquid that made all his motions languidly slow. Something was roaring behind him, getting louder, catching up to him. When he tried to look over his shoulder, all he could see was a giant pair of hands reaching for him.

He tried to run faster, but couldn't. The roaring became ear-shattering. Lightning crashed and the hands grabbed at him, caught him, bore him down, pushed him under, beat at him, pummeled him. He couldn't breathe, couldn't even scream. . . .

He woke up, wide-eyed and drenched with sweat, trembling. Half a meter above his face was the curving ceiling of the underground shelter. In the bunk below him he could hear Cranston snoring lightly. The hum of electrical machinery was the only other sound, beside his own throbbing pulsebeat.

The wind had died!

Dan pushed himself up to a sitting position, and his back muscles screamed agony. For a moment he was dizzy. Forcing both the pain and faintness down, he swung his legs slowly over the edge of the bunk and slid down to the plastic flooring. The jolt when his feet hit the floor sent a fresh spark of pain shooting through him.

He shook Cranston awake.

"Huh . . . whuzzit . . ."

"I think the storm's over," Dan said. "You try the radio while I get suited up."

Cranston swung out of the bunk slowly. For a long moment he sat on its edge, head drooping tiredly.

"What . . . how . . . what time's it?"

Dan glanced at his wristwatch. It was set on ship time. "We must've slept more than twelve hours. Come on, try the radio."

"How d'you feel?" Cranston asked as he pulled himself to his feet.

"Black and blue all over. Otherwise okay."

"It's this damned gravity."

Cranston shuffled over to the little desk that bore the communications transceiver, minus viewscreen. As he flicked it on and started talking into the speaker, Dan pulled on the one usable pressure suit they had left.

By the time Dan was checking the seal of his helmet, he could hear Cranston saying, "No use. Can't get through to them. No answer."

"Interference from the storm?"

The computerman shook his head. "Not much static. Just silence. I don't think this set has enough muscle to reach the ship without the main antenna and the amplifier up in the tent."

Dan said nothing. He clumped to the airlock, stepped through it, and shut the inner hatch. The airlock cycled through, pumping all its air into storage tanks, then flashed the green "all clear" light.

Dan reached up and unsealed the outer hatch. He pushed it upward, and a fine powder of yellowish sand and ash trickled down onto his faceplate.

Stepping up the rungs of the metal ladder set into the airlock's wall, Dan pushed the outside hatch all the way open and stuck his head up above the opening.

The camp looked as if it had been bombed. The tent was completely gone, not a shred of it left. The desks and consoles and other gear from inside the tent were nowhere in sight, either. Nothing there but the plastisteel foundation, and even that was buried under several centimeters of powdery sand and ash.

The sky overhead was gray now, sullen-looking. The clouds were high, but moving with great speed. Dan turned stiffly with the suit and tried to look in all directions. No break in the clouds anywhere: gray from horizon to horizon.

The refinery was a complete shambles. The big cylinders and spheres were cracked open, blackened and burned. *Not much to salvage from it,* Dan realized. He knew he should have been glad just to be alive, but somehow he felt terribly dejected, defeated, let down.

The communications mast was gone, of course. So were most of the trees. The grass was still there, though, poking through the sand and ash, its cheerful yellow strangely incongruous in the somber scene of destruction.

Dan stepped down the ladder again, lowering the

hatch after him. He sealed it, set the airlock to recycling again; the native sulfurous air was pumped outside, the breathable air that had been stored away hissed out of the tanks and filled the tiny airlock once again. When the light flashed green, Dan opened the inner hatch and stepped back into the main area of the shelter.

He took off his helmet. It felt as if it weighed a ton.

Cranston was still seated in front of the radio. "No response. We can't reach them."

"They can't see us, either," Dan said grimly. "Cloud deck's still covering us."

"Isn't there any way we can tell them we're here? Can't they spot us with radar or infrared or something?"

Dan plopped on the lower bunk and reached for the zips on his suit legs. "Radar won't tell them if we're alive or not. But if we could make a big enough hot spot, IR might pick it up. . . ."

"A hot spot. With what?"

Dan shrugged. "I don't think we've got anything bigger than the suit lasers. That won't do."

"Uhmm . . ." Cranston started to look concerned. "How much air and water do we have?"

"We pull our oxygen out of the planet's air," Dan answered. "Clean out the sulfur and other gunk so we can breathe it. That's no problem. Water, though . . . our water purification gear was all topside. It's gone. . . . There's probably not more than a couple days' worth in here."

"And how long will the clouds cover us?"

Dan shrugged. "Maybe we ought to try to figure out how to make a big hot spot."

Larry was pacing back and forth along the bridge, followed by Joe Haller and Guido Estelella. The technicians working the various consoles kept their faces turned very carefully to their work.

"But you can't let them sit down there without even trying to pick them up!" Haller was shouting.

Larry whirled and pointed to one of the viewscreens. It showed nothing but gray cloud scudding across the planet's face.

"There's absolutely no evidence that they're still alive," he snapped back, lower-keyed but still with an edge of anger to his voice. "You want me to risk our only qualified pilot and our only landing shuttle on the chance that they might have survived the storm?"

"Hell yes!"

"I'm willing to try it," Estelella said.

Larry shook his head. "We have no idea of what conditions are like under those clouds. The whole surface could be buried under tons of volcanic ash."

"We have other landing shuttles," Haller insisted. "You can order them taken out of the storage depot and reassembled."

"Can I replace our one qualified astronaut?" Larry demanded.

"But he's volunteered to go!"

"No." Larry pushed past Haller and started pacing the bridge again.

Haller followed doggedly. "You're killing two men!"

"They're already dead," Larry said. "We'd have heard from them by now if they were still alive. The storm's been over nearly two days."

"Their communications gear might've been damaged. They could be hurt, trapped in wreckage . . . anything."

Larry countered, "Nothing survived that storm. You saw the electrical signals we were getting from the lightning. Like a continuous sheet of flame. The wind speeds were right off the scale of our meteorological instruments. Those clouds are still moving at fifty kilometers an hour. How do we know what the wind and weather conditions are like under the clouds?"

Haller's shoulders slumped. "How much longer are the clouds supposed to last?"

"Nobody knows," Larry said. "They're coming from the chain of volcanoes on the other side of the sea. It might end in a few hours or a few weeks. Nobody knows."

"So we're just going to sit here and wait."

"That's all we can do."

Haller looked as if he wanted to say something more, but instead he turned abruptly away from Larry and marched off the bridge. Estelella stood there for a puzzled moment, then, with a shrug, he walked off too.

Larry turned to the viewscreens showing the planet's surface. Gray clouds covered almost everything. He shook his head. *They're dead,* he told himself. *They must be dead.*

But if they're not, he knew, *you're killing them.*

Abruptly, he went over to one of the technicians and said, "I'm leaving the bridge. Take over for me."

The girl looked up at him, surprised. "Where will you be?"

"You can reach me on the intercom. Page me, if you need me."

Larry ducked through the doorway into the corridor that connected to his office. He hesitated for just a moment, then entered the compartment. Without bothering to slide the door shut, he went to the phone and punched it on savagely.

"Get Valery Loring here, right away."

The computer's voice said calmly, "Working."

Valery appeared at his door ten agonized minutes later. Larry was still fidgeting beside his desk when she arrived.

"You sent for me?"

He wanted to reach out and hold her. Instead, he said flatly, "They think I want to kill Dan."

"Who does?"

Larry saw his hands flutter angrily. "Haller, Estelella, the whole damned crew on the bridge, for all I know."

Standing uncertainly by the door, Valery asked, "Do you want to kill him?"

"No! Of course not! What kind of a question is that?"

"Then why are you afraid of what they think?"

"You don't understand," he said quietly. "None of you understands at all."

"Understands what, Larry?"

"I'm the Chairman. Can't you see what that means? I have to decide. Me. My decision. Life or death. I have to decide on sending Estelella down there . . . maybe getting him killed. Or forcing him to stay aboard ship while we can't tell for certain what the surface conditions are. And that'll probably kill Dan, if he isn't dead already."

"There's still no word from him?"

"Nothing. We've been scanning the area with every instrument we've got. No indication that they survived. Nothing at all."

"They could be in the shelter."

"I know." He pulled out the desk chair and sank into it. Valery remained standing by the door.

"I have to decide," Larry repeated.

"Does Estelella want to try a landing?" she asked.

"Yes. But it's my decision to make, not his."

"I know. I wish there was some way I could help you."

"Nobody can help."

She took an uncertain step into the tiny office. "Larry . . . what do you *want* to do?"

He stared at her. The answer was obvious to him. "I want to send Estelella down there and see if they're still alive. Do you think I want to kill Dan?"

She said, "I think you want to do what's right, but you're letting your responsibilities as Chairman get in the way of your best judgment."

"But suppose he wrecks the shuttle? Suppose he's killed trying to land? We don't know very much about the conditions down there. . . ."

"He's volunteered to try," Val answered. "You want to try it. Even if he's killed, at least you'll both have tried. It's better than sitting around and doing nothing, isn't it? If you don't try, we know Dan will die. But if you do try . . ."

He nodded unhappily. "You're right . . . they all know . . ."

"There's something that *I* know," Valery said.

"What is it?"

"I know that no matter what's happened . . . or what's

going to happen . . . you'd never willingly hurt anyone. Not even Dan."

"He . . . he was my best friend. We were all friends, once."

"A million years ago." Val's voice was faint and distant.

Larry took a deep breath. Standing, he said, "All right, we'll try it. But I'm riding down with Estelella myself."

Valery didn't seem surprised. "There's no need for that. You don't have to prove anything. Not to me or anyone else."

"No, I want to do it."

"But you can't. You're the Chairman. And besides, you'd only be wasting valuable mass and space aboard the shuttle. There's nothing you can do to help . . . except to make the right decision."

Dan was standing out on the surface in the protective suit. His face was haggard, with several days' worth of dark scrubby beard mottling his chin. His mouth was caked and dry.

He was staring at the sea, only a few hundred meters from the wrecked base, where he stood. The waves were lapping up softly, sliding up onto the sandy beach. He could walk out there and be waist-deep in the water . . .

Can't drink it, he was telling himself. *It's got to be purified. The contaminants in it will kill you.*

"Another few hours," he mumbled, his voice thick and raspy, "and it won't make any difference what's in the water. We'll have to try it."

Cranston was back in the shelter, in his bunk, para-

lyzed by the fear of dying. Dan found that he couldn't
stand being in the cramped little shelter with him. It was
better up here on the surface, even though he had to stay
inside the suit. His own body smell was getting overpowering, though.

He almost smiled. *Larry's going to get his way, after
all. I can just see him. Death-planet, he'll call it. Too dangerous. Got to move on.* The smile faded. *He's going to
make sure we die.*

A distant crack of thunder and its following rumble
made him look up. Another storm? No, the sky looked the
same as it had for the past three days: gray, completely
overcast, but not stormy. The wind was so light that he
couldn't notice it except as a gentle swaying of the grass.

Dan looked up again. And blinked. There was a white
streak etching across the clouded sky. A thin white line.
A contrail!

If he could have jumped inside the heavy suit, he
would have. He wanted to leap up and down, to dance,
to shout.

Instead he stood rooted to the spot, watching as the
streak swung around overhead. He could make out the
tiny arrowhead form of the shuttle rocket now. It grew,
took on solidity. The sweetly beautiful roar of the craft's
auxiliary turbo engines came to him, even through the
helmet and earphones. The ship banked smoothly, raced
low across the water and came up toward him, landing
wheels out. It touched down with a puff of dust, rolled
past the ruined base.

Dan stood there motionless as the shuttle craft taxied

around, nosed back toward the base and edged slowly toward him, engines screeching and blowing up a miniature sandstorm of dust and ash behind it.

Then the roar died away. The bubble canopy popped open and a pressure-suited figure stood up.

In sudden realization, Dan reached for the radio switch on his belt.

". . . just stand there, will you? Say something, wave, *do something!* What's the matter, are you frozen?"

"I'm okay," Dan croaked, his voice sounding strange and harsh, even to himself. "Just . . . thirsty."

"You're alive!" It was Estelella's voice, and there was no missing the elation in it. "Don't move . . . I've got plenty of water with me. Be right there."

If Dan had still had enough moisture in his body, he would have cried for joy.

They celebrated that night.

Nearly everyone on the ship, all those who weren't absolutely needed on duty, gathered in the cafeteria and ate and drank and sang together. Dan had to fight off the determined medical insistence of the whole infirmary staff, but he made the scene too. In a wheelchair.

"It's my party, dammit!" he shouted at them.

For the first time in months, Dan, Valery, and Larry found themselves at the same place, even at the same table. And for a few hours, it was almost like old times. No one mentioned Larry's reluctance to send a ship down to the surface. Old tensions, old fears were forgotten. For a while.

They laughed together, remembered happier times. They sang far into the early hours of the morning.

But then, as the party was finally winding down and people were tiptoeing or staggering or lurching homeward, somebody said loudly enough for everyone to hear:

"I guess this proves that we can't stay on the surface. Too dangerous. We were lucky to get you guys back alive."

Dan's face went deathly grim. "It proves that we need much better equipment and precautions to work on the surface. But if we lived through that storm, we can live through whatever else the planet throws at us."

"I don't know . . ." Larry began.

Valery said, "We still need more deuterium, don't we? Someone will have to go back to the surface, with more equipment."

"That'll be a long, tough job."

"But it's got to be done."

Dan pushed himself out of the wheelchair and got to his feet. He still looked gaunt, eyes dark and haggard. "We can do what needs to be done. And our children, when they've been specially adapted for life on the surface, will make that planet their playground."

Larry glanced at Val. She was looking up at Dan. And the only thing he felt in his heart was hatred.

Chapter 14

It was the next morning when Dan tracked down Valery in the ship's library.

She was sitting in one of the small tape-reading booths. There were two viewscreens mounted side by side on the booth wall, and Val was comparing some of the spectrograms she had made with the big telescope against the spectral analysis charts in the library's files.

Dan tapped on the glass door of the booth. She turned, smiled, and waved him in.

He slid the door open and squeezed into the booth. There was only one chair, and hardly enough room for him to stand beside her. The door slid shut automatically as soon as he let go of it.

"Cozy in here," he said, grinning.

"It's not built for comfort," Valery agreed, shifting her weight slightly on the stiff metal chair.

"I wanted to know if you're free for dinner tonight?" His voice rose enough to make it a question.

Val shook her head.

"Lunch?"

"Dan," she said sadly. "I told you and Larry the same thing. Until the two of you stop fighting each other, I'm

not going to have much to do with either of you. I won't
be the bait in a battle between you."

"But you said . . ."

"I've said a lot of things. Now I'm saying that the answer to both of you is *no* . . . as long as you're fighting
each other."

"But Larry is . . ."

"I don't want to hear it."

Dan could feel hot anger rising inside him.

She almost smiled at him. "You don't have to look so
grim."

"Don't I?"

"No. . . . Look, here are some of the results of the
spectra I've taken with the main telescope. I haven't
shown them to anybody else, but I'll show them to you."

He shrugged. "Big thrill."

"Don't be fresh. And you've got to promise not to tell
anyone until I make my report to the Council next week.
I don't want these data leaking out before I've had a
chance to check everything through thoroughly."

"I can keep a secret," Dan said tightly.

"Well . . ." Val lowered her voice to almost a whisper.
"Both stars seem to have Earthlike planets."

"What?"

Nodding, Val went on, her voice rising with excitement. "Epsilon Indi is the closer of the two stars, so I can
resolve its planets more easily. Not that I've been able to
see anything except a pinpoint of light, even with the
best image intensification. But the gravimetric measurements look good, and the spectral data . . ."

She turned to the twin viewscreens. "Look . . . here's a spectrum I made twenty-four hours ago of the innermost planet of Epsilon Indi—the one that's about Earth's size and mass. And here, on the other screen, is a spectrum I made of Earth with the same telescope, a few days earlier. We're just about the same distance from both planets —about four lightyears."

Dan squinted at the two viewscreens. Each showed a smear of colors, crisscrossed by hundreds of dark lines. The Earth spectrum seemed to be dominated by shades of yellow, while the Epsilon Indi spectrum seemed more orange.

"The background continuum isn't what's important," Valery explained. "Look at the absorption lines. . . ." She pointed from one viewscreen to the other. "Oxygen . . . here. And here. Nitrogen, on both. Water vapor . . . carbon dioxide," her slim hand kept shifting back and forth, "and all at just about the same concentration. It's fantastic!"

"You mean this planet's just like Earth?"

"So close to each other that it's hard to tell where they're different, from this distance, at least."

"But . . ." Dan's insides were churning now. "But, the Epsilon Indi planet is just as far from us now as Earth and the solar system."

"Yes, that's true," Val admitted.

"We could never make it there."

Instead of answering, Valery turned back to the keyboard in front of the viewscreens. One of the pictures disappeared, to be replaced by another spectrogram.

"This is the spectrum of Femina . . . it's much more intense than the Epsilon Indi planet's, because we're right next to it."

"And the other spectrogram is still Earth's?"

"Yes," Val said. "And look at the differences in the atmospheric constituents. Sulfur oxides, big gobs of carbon dioxide and monoxide, other things I haven't even identified yet."

Even Dan's unpracticed eye could see that the two spectrograms were very different from each other.

"Considering what you went through down there on the surface," Valery said, "I should think you'd want to repair the ship and then push on for Epsilon Indi."

Dan said nothing. He leaned against the acoustically insulated wall of the tiny booth; his face was pale, his eyes troubled.

"Thanks for showing me," he said quietly. "I . . . won't tell anybody until you give your report at the Council meeting."

And then he pulled the door open and stepped out of the booth, leaving Valery there alone to watch him walking quickly through the tape shelves of the library.

Now I've told each of them the exact opposite of what he wants to hear, she thought. *Which one will come after me and try to silence me before the Council meeting?*

Four days passed.

Larry sat in the main conference room, at his usual chair at the head of the table. But the table was mostly empty. Only Dan, Dr. Polanyi, Mort Campbell, and Guido Estelella were there, all clustered up close to Larry's seat.

"From everything you've been telling me," Larry was saying, looking at the chart on the viewscreen at the far end of the long, narrow room, "we have no choice but to go down to the surface again and try to repair the refining equipment."

Polanyi folded his hands over his paunchy middle and agreed. "Whether we eventually decide to stay here or to move on, we still must have enough deuterium for many more years of living aboard the ship."

"And we've got to overhaul just about everything on board," Campbell added. "Doesn't make a bit of difference if we're going to live here or find another planet. The ship's starting to fall apart. We've got to patch her up."

Larry turned to Estelella. "What about rebuilding the refining equipment? That'll take a lot of shuttling back and forth to the surface."

The astronaut tilted his head slightly to one side. "That's what I'm here for. . . . I'm no use to anyone just sitting around."

"No, I suppose not," Larry said seriously. "How many flights will be necessary? Will you have to do all the flying yourself or will some of the other kids you've been training be able to help?"

"There are at least three or four who can fly the shuttle almost as well as I can," Estelella said. It could have sounded like a boast, but he said it as a simple statement of fact. "And we can take the back-up shuttles out of storage and use them, too."

Larry nodded thoughtfully.

"I think," Dan said, "it'd be a good idea to have a spare

shuttle on the ground next to the camp at all times. That way we'll always have an escape route, in an emergency."

"Good idea," Larry said.

"The only real danger on the surface that we've run into are the storms," Estelella muttered.

Polanyi said, "They appear to be tied in with the volcanic disturbances. If we could revive our full meteorological and geological teams, perhaps we could get accurate predictions of when to expect storms . . ."

Larry cut him off. "We can't revive large numbers of people until we've made a firm decision to stay here. And that decision won't be made until we get a full report on the other available planets."

"We're still going to be orbiting *this* planet," Dan argued, "for a long time. Years, maybe."

The others nodded agreement.

Dan went on, "I'm going down there with the first crew . . . got to see how bad the damage to the refinery really is."

"You just got back," Larry said. "And the medics are still . . ."

"I'm responsible for the equipment," Dan snapped, his voice rising a notch louder than Larry's. "It's my job. I'm going down."

Larry forced down an urge to shout back at him. "All right," he said coldly, "then the only question is, when do we start?"

"Sooner the better," Dan said.

"The campsite is in darkness now," Estelella said, with a glance at his wristwatch. "It'll be daylight there again in about . . . eight hours."

"That puts it close to midnight, ship time."

"Right."

Dan said, "Let's get a landing group together and get down there as soon as there's enough light to see."

"We can take off at midnight," Estelella said.

"Good. You, me, and enough equipment to get the camp started again. Who else will we need?"

Larry was getting that helpless feeling again. Dan was running things his own way.

"You'd both better get some sleep," he said. "And I'll get the maintenance crew to crack the back-up shuttles out of storage, so you can get them into action as soon as possible."

"Right."

They got up from their chairs and headed for the door. Larry was the last to reach the doorway. Dan was still there, lingering, waiting for him.

"You're not fooling me," Dan said.

Larry frowned at him. "What do you mean?"

"You don't have any intention of staying here. I know that. You're going to get the ship overhauled and patched up, and then try to convince everybody we ought to push on."

To where? Larry almost said. But he wouldn't give Dan the satisfaction. Instead, he asked, "You enjoyed your trip to the surface so much? You think it's a fun place to be?"

"It's better than this ship."

Larry snorted. "That's like saying that death is better than life."

"Wrong!" Dan snapped. "Can't you see it's wrong? This

is where we have to stay. Trying to push farther is just going to kill everybody! Is that what you want?"

"We've had this argument before, Dan."

"You're still not convinced?"

"This planet is a killer," Larry said. "We can alter the next generation or two or even three . . . but I still don't think they'll be able to survive on Femina. The planet's deadly: Guido picked a good name for it."

Dan started to answer, but Larry went on, "It's a huge universe out there. It would be criminal of us to settle for this planet when there've got to be better worlds for us. Somewhere. There's got to be."

"We'll see" Dan said, his voice shaking. "We'll see. And soon."

Midnight.

There was no way to distinguish time on the bridge. Along the ship's corridors and tubes, in the rec areas and cafeteria, the overhead lighting was dimmed during the night shifts. But in the working spaces, such as the bridge, everything looked the same whether it was midnight or noon. Only the people working changed. And the twenty-four-hour clocks.

Larry stood behind the launch monitor, watching over his shoulders the viewscreens that showed the planet below them and the shuttle rocket sitting on the ship's launching platform, up near the hub.

The campsite was in daylight now; under the highest magnification of the observation scopes, Larry could see a blackened smudge where the camp had been.

He turned to the screen that showed the shuttle craft.

He could make out the two pressure-suited men sitting side by side in the pilot's bubble. Estelella's voice was checking off the countdown routine:

"Internal power on."

". . . nine, eight, seven . . ."

"Rockets armed and ready for ignition."

". . . five, four . . ."

"Tracking and telemetry on," said a technician.

". . . two, one, *zero*."

The electric catapult slid the shuttle craft out past the open airlock hatch. Larry watched the viewscreen. It showed the shuttle dwindling, dwindling, becoming one more speck among the endless stars.

"Rocket ignition," came Estelella's voice.

The speck blossomed briefly into a glow of light. Then even that disappeared.

"Tracking on the observation telescope," said a tech.

Larry turned toward the sound of her voice. The main screen on her console showed the shuttle craft, a tiny red-glowing meteor streaking across the broad golden landscape of the planet.

"Telemetry and voice communications strong and clear."

Larry pressed the shoulder of the tech he was standing behind. "I'm going to my quarters to grab some sleep. Call me when they've landed."

He stepped out of the glare and bustle of the bridge, into the soft shadowy nighttime lighting of the corridors. His own room was dark. He didn't bother turning on a light, just slouched onto the bunk and waited.

The phone chimed. He touched the VOICE ONLY button.

"Yes?"

"They've landed. Estelella reports all okay, they're getting out of the shuttle and starting to look around."

"Thank you."

Larry sat on the bunk, motionless, for a long while. Then he turned to the phone again. "Valery Loring, please."

A pause. *Of course. She's asleep by now.*

Mrs. Loring's face appeared on the viewscreen. "Larry, is that you? I can hardly see you. Don't you have any lights on?"

"I'm sorry to wake you," he said. "Is Val there?"

"I wasn't asleep," she said. "Haven't been sleeping well lately . . ." Her voice trailed off. Then, "Valery's up in the observatory. She's been keeping very odd hours lately."

"Oh. All right. Thank you. I'll call her there."

But he knew he wasn't going to call her on the phone. He had to go up there and see her, face to face.

Two more nights, Valery was thinking. *Two more nights, and then on the third morning the Council meets. Then I'll have to tell them all the truth.*

Each night for the past week she had been staying up in the observatory, sitting at the desk her father had used. The myriads of stars sprinkled across the blackness outside seemed to make the place feel colder, lonelier. Their light brought no warmth. The huge bulk of the planet was out of sight, down below the floor of the observatory, on the other side of the ship.

The big spidery telescope bulked blackly against the

stars, and the smaller pieces of equipment made a hodge-podge of shadows. Black on black. Dark and darker. Only the little glowlights from the computer terminal and the viewscreens lit Val's post.

She tried to stay awake through each night, of course. She actually got quite a bit of work done. But for long stretches of the night the telescopes and cameras and other instruments were doing their tasks and there was almost nothing for her to do. Except think. And—too often—drift into sleep, lulled by the weightlessness of the observatory and the silence.

Click!

She tensed instantly.

The sound of a hatch opening. Val strained her eyes, but could see nothing in the darkness. There were several hatches leading into the observatory, and with the tubes on nighttime lights, there wouldn't be much of a glow to see when one of them was opened.

Padding footsteps. Slippered feet walking softly across the observatory floor.

"Who's there?" she called.

No answer.

Dan went out on the shuttle, she knew.

"Larry, it's you, isn't it?"

His lean dark form seemed to coalesce out of the shadows. "Yes," he said quietly, not five meters away from her. "It's me."

Her pulse was racing. "Oh . . . you scared me . . . a little."

"I didn't mean to."

He was close enough now for her to see his face in the

glow of the desk lights. He looked infinitely weary. He pulled up a chair and floated softly onto it. Valery noticed that he didn't snap on the zero-g restraining belt. As calmly and unhurriedly as she could, she unclipped her own lap belt. It clicked loudly and snapped back into its resting sockets.

"Why . . . what brings you up here?" she asked.

For a moment he didn't answer, merely stared at her. "I just had to talk to somebody," he said at last. "I . . . lately, I've had the feeling that I'm completely alone. Totally cut off from everybody. No friends, nobody."

"I'm still your friend, Larry," she said softly.

"It's hard for us to be friends, Val. After everything that's happened . . . we can't be friends. Not really."

"I don't understand."

He seemed miserable. "Can't you see? When you tell the Council that you haven't been able to find an Earthlike planet, they're going to vote to stay here. They'll elect Dan Chairman and the geneticists will be put to work preparing the next generation of children for that deathworld down there. *Your* children, Val! Yours and Dan's. They'll be monsters. Sulfur-breathing, gorilla-sized monsters."

She had to struggle to keep her voice from shaking. "But what else can we do?"

"We've got to keep on going. Got to find an Earthlike planet somewhere. In this whole universe . . ."

"There might not be any," Valery said. "Maybe Earth is a unique place. Why should we expect anything closer to Earth conditions than the planet down below us?"

Larry didn't answer. He just sat there and lifted his

head back, gazing up at the stars that crowded all around.

"I can see why you like it up here," he said. "It's peaceful here. Like being alone in the universe . . . floating free among the stars. It wouldn't be a bad way to die, just floating out there. No cares, no weight, just out there in the universe, without the ship to hem you in."

"Wh . . . what do you mean?"

He snapped his attention back to her. Valery felt a chill as his ice-blue eyes focused on her.

"You got Dr. Hsai to start revival procedures on a team of psychiatrists," Larry said flatly.

"I . . . we talked about it, yes . . ."

"Why?" Larry asked, rising up from his chair like a ghost. "I told Hsai it wasn't necessary. Why did you get him to countermand my decision?"

"He thought it would be best," Valery said, her voice going high, the words coming out fast. "I didn't tell him to do it; he decided for himself."

"He didn't decide until after you talked to him." He was standing over her now, feet barely touching the floor, looming over her.

Valery got up from her chair, bumping Larry slightly so that he bobbed away gently.

"Larry . . . you and Dan are both certain that there's a madman aboard the ship. A killer. You think it's Dan and he thinks it's you."

"So?"

Carefully, Val edged over in front of the desk and sat on it. Her feet no longer touched the floor. She gripped the edge of the desk with both hands.

"So shouldn't we have a psychiatrist on hand to examine him? And—and you?"

"Me? Why me? I'm not the killer!"

Suddenly Val didn't know how to say what she knew had to be said. She plunged ahead anyway.

"Larry—have you ever thought that maybe, if Dan is the killer, he doesn't know it?"

"Huh?"

"He might be doing things that his conscious mind isn't aware of. And, besides, he hasn't killed anybody. Not really."

"He tried to kill your father. And the fire in the cryonics unit might have been deliberately set. That's still a possibility."

"All right," Valery said, inching the top desk drawer open with her right hand. "Even if he did . . . maybe he doesn't know about it. He might be sick, insane."

"That doesn't mean he's not dangerous."

"I know," Val agreed. "But—you can understand that he might be doing all these things without being consciously aware of it."

Looking puzzled now, Larry said, "Yes . . . I guess that's possible."

Val held her breath for an instant, then blurted, "Then you can see that it might be *you* who's doing it! You could be the sick one and not even know it!"

"Whhaaat?"

Larry's eyes went wide with shock. He seemed to stagger back.

"No!" he roared. "That can't be!"

Tears were springing up in Val's eyes, and her vision

was getting blurry. "Larry, it could be. It could be!"

"You're wrong. That's crazy . . . it's not me. . . ."

Her hand closed on the cold hard metal she was seeking.

"Why did you come up here tonight?" Val asked. "Why did you come up here the night my father was nearly killed?"

"No!" he shouted again, and started for her.

Valery pulled the sonic stunner out of the desk drawer and fired point-blank. The gun made a barely-audible popping sound. But Larry's body stiffened, his eyes glazed, his arms froze outstretched barely a few centimeters from her. He didn't fall, he couldn't in zero-gravity. He merely hung there, unconscious.

Val found that her hands were shaking wildly now, and she was sobbing.

Then:

"Very neat work. The two of you are being very cooperative."

Dan Christopher stepped out of the shadows from beyond the desk, grinning.

Chapter 15

Valery blinked back her tears.

"Dan! But I thought you . . ."

He was still some distance away from the desk, just close enough to be seen as a tall, lithe shadow. "That was Joe Haller on the shuttle. I asked him to take my place at the last minute."

"What . . . what are you doing here?"

"The same thing I tried to do when your father first started this nonsense of looking for another planet."

Val felt completely confused. "But . . . I thought . . ."

Dan laughed. "You made just about every mistake you could make, Val. You thought it was Larry, when all along it's been me."

"You're the madman?" The question popped out of her involuntarily.

Still hovering off near the shadows, Dan said grimly, "Wrong again. I'm not insane. It's not insanity when you fight to protect yourself from your so-called friends. Not when they're laughing at you behind your back. Plotting against you. Taking everything away from you."

"I . . . never laughed at you, Dan."

"Not much." His voice was getting hard, steel-edged. "You talked Larry into the Chairmanship. You probably got him to kill my father. Don't tell me the two of you weren't laughing at me."

"Dan, you're wrong . . . can't you see?"

"I see perfectly. I've seen it all along. You kill my father. While I'm mourning him, Larry takes over the Chairmanship and you take over Larry. Then the two of you scheme to move the ship on to another planet, another star. Not where we're *supposed* to go, where we're *destined* to go. Oh no! You've got to have your way in everything, don't you?"

Valery realized she still held the stunner in her hand. "Dan, it isn't like that at all."

"You even got your father to help you, didn't you?" he went on. "Searching for other planets. I fixed him. But you wouldn't let it rest there. Now I've got to take care of you, too. . . ." His voice seemed to break.

"Dan? Dan, please."

"No," he said, almost sobbing. "Val, I loved you. I would have given my life for you. But you've always been against me. You've always loved Larry better than me. You've all been against me, all along."

"Dan, you're wrong. Come here," she gripped the stunner firmly, "and let me prove how wrong you are."

"Sure, I'll come to you." His voice grew stronger. "As soon as you toss that popgun away."

Valery brought it up to fire, but Dan melted into the shadows before she could pull the trigger.

"It's a very short-range weapon," she heard his voice call to her, echoing mockingly. "And very directional. Now this laser I borrowed from the pressure suit is only a working tool . . . but at this distance it can burn your arm off the shoulder."

A blood-red pencil-beam of energy shot past Valery's ear.

She screamed and jumped, hitting the edge of the desk with her legs.

"The next one won't miss, Val. Throw your gun away."

She tossed it from her. The gun went spinning weightlessly into the darkness.

Dan stepped closer, close enough for her to see his face in the faint glow of the desk lights. He didn't look wild-eyed or twisted at all. He seemed perfectly at ease, calmer than usual. Serene.

"What are you going to do?" she asked.

"What can I do?" he shot back. "You've left me no alternative. For a while, I tried to figure out some way of getting you to agree to cryosleep, so I wouldn't have to kill you. But that's not possible. Not now."

"Dan, you've got to stop. You can't kill everyone that . . ."

"Everyone that gets in my way? Everyone who takes what's rightfully mine? Yes, I can kill them all. You just watch me do it."

"You're sick!"

"Sick of being cheated by those who claim they love me." He gestured with the laser pistol. "Erase all your data tapes."

"I . . ." Val's mind was racing. "If I do, will you let me live?"

"That's impossible."

"I'll go into cryosleep. You can take me down there yourself. Right away."

He hesitated a moment. "Erase the tapes."

She turned and flicked her fingers over the keyboard. Lights on the computer terminal's face flickered on and off.

Turning back to Dan she said, "Well? You don't have to kill anyone."

Dan glanced at Larry's inert form. "You want me to let him be frozen, too?"

"Yes."

"So the two of you can awake together? Never," Dan said firmly. "He killed my father."

"No one killed your father," Valery said, her voice rising. "It was an accident."

"Don't argue with me!" he shouted. "He killed my father and I'm going to kill him. He's always been after everything that's mine. Now he's going to pay for it."

"Then you'll have to kill me too!" Val shouted back.

He pointed the gun at her. Val slid sideways, away from the computer terminal. "Look!" she yelled. "It's not on erase, it's on *record*! And I put the intercom on, too. Everything you've said for the past minute or two is being broadcast all over the ship. There must be an emergency crew heading up here right now!"

"You . . ." Now Dan's eyes glittered dangerously, and his breath became ragged, gulping.

"It won't do you any good to kill us, Dan," Val said as calmly as she could manage. "Everyone knows now. Just give up and let the medics take care of you."

With a bellowing roar, Dan fired the laser into the

computer terminal. It exploded in a shower of sparks. Valery leaped upward as the desk lights blanked out, then angled to one side and desperately tried to put as much distance between herself and Dan as she could.

"I'll get you!" He was screaming. "Both of you! All of you!"

Larry! Somewhere in the vast, completely darkened chamber, Larry's unconscious body floated. If Dan found him first . . . Valery saw a gaunt framework of shadows moving up toward her. The main telescope. She put out both hands and grabbed at one of the girders, slowing her impact.

Hanging there weightlessly, she peered into the darkness, letting her eyes adjust to the dim starlight. *There.* A body floating silently off in the distance. *Is it Larry, or a trick of Dan's?*

The click and creak of a hatch opening made her turn her attention toward the sound. A shaft of light flickered through the observatory, and Valery caught the shadow of Dan's form squeezing down through the hatch, then slamming it shut behind him.

She launched herself across the room toward Larry. Another hatch opened, off to the other side of the observatory, and a man's voice called out:

"Miss Loring, are you all right?"

"I'm here! Get some lights and help me. Larry Belsen's unconscious."

Talk about irony, Larry thought.

He was sitting in Dan's desk chair in the Propulsion and Power control center, one level below the observatory. The gravity was still low enough for his arms to tend to float up off the chair arms. Someone was holding a vibrator to the back of his neck, soothing away the roaring headache that the stunner had given hin.

Valery was standing in front of him, looking very pale and frightened.

Half a dozen engineers and technicians were at their stations. All of them wore stunners on their belts.

"How does your head feel now?" a girl's voice came from behind him.

Too stiff and aching to turn toward her, he replied, "Like somebody's running a rocket engine inside it."

The girl moved in front of him, where he could see that she was wearing a white nurse's coverall. "I'll get you a pain-killer." She opened a kit on the desk.

Larry looked up at Valery. "So you thought it was me."

Her eyes were red from crying, he noticed.

"I was *afraid* it was you," she answered quietly.

"Do you feel any better," he asked bitterly, "knowing that it's Dan?"

"Not much," she confessed. Then she added, "But . . . I'm glad it wasn't you. Even if you'd been doing it unconsciously."

The nurse turned back to him and handed him an immense blue pill.

"I'll get some water," Valery said.

"Make it a bucketful," Larry called to her. To the nurse, he asked, "Will this make me sleep?"

She shook her head. "No, it's a selective depressant. If you want to sleep . . ."

"No, I've got to stay awake."

Val came back with a plastic cup of water. Larry swallowed hard on the pill, nearly choked, but finally forced it down.

"Any idea of where Dan is?" he asked.

Val said, "No. Mort Campbell is heading up the emergency squad. They're searching the ship for him."

"Could you get Mort on the phone for me, please?"

She handled the desk phone, while Larry rubbed the back of his still stiff neck.

Campbell's heavy-featured face showed up on the screen.

"Where are you?" Larry asked.

"Storage area seventeen. One of the maintenance men working on the extra shuttles said he heard some strange noises down here."

"Anything?"

Campbell's beefy face settled into a scowl. "Who knows? This area's big enough to hide the whole ship's crew. We've got kilometers of corridors and tubes to search, thousands of sections and compartments . . . a few dozen men can't hack it. Not even a few hundred."

"He's got to be someplace. I'll make sure that all the working and living areas are guarded. He'll have to show up sooner or later . . . even if it's just to get some food."

"I know. But I wouldn't count on that. Anyway, there are video monitors on all the important areas of the ship. I've got a special squad of people monitoring the viewscreens on the bridge."

"Good."

Campbell said, "I understand he's armed."

"He was. But I want him brought in alive. No rough stuff. If you have to fight, use the stunners."

"He must be really sick."

"And scared. Be careful with him. But don't take unnecessary chances; he's perfectly willing to kill."

Campbell's eyes flickered with just the barest hint of surprise. "Yeah, I guess you're right," he said.

The picture on the viewscreen faded.

Larry got to his feet. For a moment he felt a surge of dizziness. Val was beside him and he rested a hand on her shoulder.

"Come on," he said. "We can be in better touch with the whole ship down on the bridge."

"Wait a minute?" she asked. "I had an idea, while you were talking with Mr. Campbell."

"What?"

"Dr. Hsai. He's spent a lot of time examining Dan, talking with him . . ."

"And finding zero," Larry grumbled.

"Yes, but he might be able to find something in his records . . . or maybe something he'll remember . . . some clue to where Dan might be hiding, what he's doing."

Larry thought it over for half a moment. "It's worth a try." He turned to the nearest technician, who was seated at a monitoring console, watching the computer-produced graphs that gave second-by-second reports on the performance of the reactors and generators. "Your name's Peterson, isn't it?"

The blond youth smiled, obviously flattered that the Chairman knew his name. "Yessir, that's right."

"Would you please call Dr. Hsai and ask him to meet me on the bridge as soon as he can possibly get there?"

"Yessir. Right away."

The oriental psychotech was already on the bridge, waiting patiently, when Larry and Val got there. All the way down the now fully lit connector tubes, padding down those spiraling metal steps, Larry had half-expected Dan to leap out at them. No sign of him. Nor of Campbell's search parties and emergency squad.

It's a big ship, Larry reminded himself. *You could roam around for weeks without seeing another person, if you really wanted to.*

All the technicians on the bridge were wearing sidearms as they sat at their consoles. And there were two grim-faced guards scowling at the door Larry and Val stepped through.

Dr. Hsai was unarmed, of course. Larry quickly explained what he was after.

The psychotech pursed his lips thoughtfully. "I must admit that nothing comes to mind right now. But I will review all my records. Perhaps there *is* something he inadvertently revealed that will help you."

There'd better be, Larry thought. To Val, he muttered, "Dan could do a lot of damage to the ship, if he wants to."

"But all the vital areas are protected now, aren't they?"

He scanned the viewscreens and nodded. "They seem to be . . . but the ship's too big. Too many soft spots. He could cut electrical connections, air lines, water pipes . . . anything."

"Why would he do something like that?" she asked.

"How should I know?" Larry snapped. "Why would he do any of the things he's doing? He's crazy!"

She didn't respond, but her chin dropped slightly.

"I'm sorry," Larry said immediately. "I didn't mean it that way. Guess I'm getting edgy."

"I know," Valery said.

The hours wore on. Larry finally had to sleep; he couldn't stay on his feet any longer. He woke up two hours later and groggily made his way back to the bridge.

Mort Campbell was there, unshaven, bleary-eyed, sipping coffee from a steaming mug.

"Anything?" Larry asked.

"Nine dozen false alarms, that's all." Campbell sipped, then winced. "Cheez, that's hot! No . . . everybody and his brother thinks they've seen him. But none of it checks out. Wherever he's hiding, it's a good place."

Larry stood through two full shifts. Most of the time he remained on the bridge, although he put in a swing with one of Campbell's search squads, spending several hours going through corridors and unused work and storage areas. All of them were sealed tight and lay under half a century's worth of dust.

He had dinner with Val in the cafeteria.

"I'm going to assign a couple of men to guard you."

"Me?"

"He was after you, wasn't he?"

"That's only because I showed him that Epsilon Indi's closest planet is almost exactly like Earth. He wanted to destroy that evidence, to make sure we stayed here."

"Oh . . . Now he knows you were lying to him."

She grinned, a bit sheepishly. "No, I was telling him the truth. It was you that I lied to."

"What? But you said . . ."

"It was a lie," she replied. "To see if . . . well, if you were the one who'd try to . . . stop me from reporting to the Council."

Larry stared at her. "You mean there really is a planet like Earth at Epsilon Indi?"

She nodded, grinning again.

"That's fantastic! Fabulous!" Larry felt like jumping up on the cafeteria table. Then he remembered about Dan. "But I still want you guarded. He's dangerous, and he might come after you. I don't want you to be bait anymore."

"I'll be all right in my own quarters. Mother's there, and we have a phone. . . ."

"And there will be two guards with you at all times," Larry said firmly.

"At *all* times?" Her eyebrows arched coyly.

Larry put on a sour face. "They'll stay outside your door when you go home."

"But . . ."

"No arguments, or I'll make it four guards."

She put her hands up in mock surrender. "Yessir, Mr. Chairman. To hear is to obey."

"Stuff it." Now he was grinning. "Uh . . . this might not be the right time, but—well, I still love you."

"I know," she said, much more softly. "I never stopped loving you."

He leaned across the table and kissed her. Seven dozen

people in the cafeteria stopped their meals to watch, but Larry couldn't have cared less. Even if he had noticed them.

"He's got to be *someplace*," Larry fumed.

He was on the bridge again, talking to Mort Campbell, who was slumped tiredly on the chair of an unoccupied console.

"A man just can't disappear for three days," Larry insisted. "It's a big ship, but you should have been able to flush him out by now."

"I know, I feel the same way," Campbell said, nodding his heavy head. "Either he's damned clever or . . ."

"Or what?"

"Or he's got friends helping him."

Larry made a chopping motion with his hand. "No. That I can't believe. A madman aboard the ship is one thing, but other madmen to help him? No."

"He got Joe Haller to take his place on the shuttle, didn't he?"

"We've gone through all that with Joe. He had no idea of what Dan was up to. Dan asked him to fill in for him, and he did. That's all."

Campbell threw his hands up in disgust. "Then where the hell is he? Why can't we find him?"

"If I knew, Mort, I'd . . ."

"Emergency signal!" sang out one of the techs.

Larry went over to her like a shot. "What is it?"

The girl pointed to a flashing red light on the console in front of her, between two viewscreens. Her hands flew over the keyboard. One of the viewscreens brightened and showed a guard, bleeding from a gushing cut on his scalp. The blood was pouring down into his eyes.

"He . . . he's here . . ."

"What's the location?" Larry yelled at the girl.

"Airlock fourteen, level three."

Campbell bolted from his chair and dashed for the nearest door.

Larry snapped, "Hook me into the intercom."

The girl nodded and did things to her keyboard. "Okay now, sir."

Leaning over her shoulder to speak into the microphone built into the console's face, Larry said: "This is the Chairman speaking. Dan Christopher has attacked a guard at airlock fourteen, level three. All search squads converge on that location. All guard units, remain on duty at your assigned posts." He started to straighten up, then had another thought. "Dan . . . Dan Christopher. Give up, Dan. You can't win. We want to help you. Give up and you won't be hurt."

But it sounded empty even as he said it.

Larry fidgeted on the bridge for about a minute longer, then said, "I'm going up to that airlock. Relay any calls for me to that location."

He got there as the guard was being carried off to the infirmary on a stretcher. Campbell was standing inside the airlock, filling its cramped metal space with his formidable bulk. He had his hands on his hips.

Larry pushed past a dozen men and stepped through the airlock's inner hatch to squeeze in next to Campbell.

"Well, now we know where he is," Campbell said.

"What happened?"

Campbell jerked a thumb at the rack of pressure suits hanging outside the airlock, in the corridor. "He slugged the guard, took one of the suits, and went outside."

"What? You're sure?"

Nodding, Campbell answered, "Yep. Just checking the hatch here. It was open when we arrived a few minutes ago."

"He's outside?"

"He's committing suicide."

Larry thought it over for a few moments. "No. He's moving to a part of the ship where he wants to be . . . My god! He can cut open bulkheads anywhere he wants to and blow whole sections of the ship into vacuum. If he does that in the living quarters . . ."

Even Campbell's normal calm seemed shaken. "We'd better get all the living quarters on disaster alert. All hatches sealed . . ."

Larry nodded. "And guards on every airlock."

"Right. Anything else?"

"Yes. Get a squad of volunteers together. We've got to go outside after him. And I'm going with you."

Chapter 16

It was a strange, eerie feeling.

Larry had been outside the ship before, but never since they had taken up orbit around the planet. Its massive curving bulk hung over him, it seemed, close and beckoning yet somehow menacing. He felt almost as if it was going to fall on him and crush him.

He shook his head inside the suit's helmet. *You've got a job to do. No time for sightseeing.*

A dozen men had floated out of the airlock in search of Dan. A dozen men to cover the thousands of possible places where he might be lurking.

They worked with a plan in mind. They came out of one airlock at the first level, the largest of the ship's seven wheels. They spread out around the periphery of that wheel. The plan was for each man to search the area between connecting tubes. Then, if none of them found Dan, they would work their way simultaneously up each of the connector tubes to the next ring, search there, then on to the third ring. And so on, right up to the hub.

We could use a hundred men, Larry thought. Only twelve men qualified for outside work had volunteered. Most of the people aboard the ship had never been outside it.

Larry watched the man nearest him disappear over the curve of the ship's ring-like structure. He was alone now, standing on the ring's metal skin with magnetically gripping boots, looking down a connector tube, past the seven rings to the bulging plastiglass blisters of the hub.

The stars formed a solemn, unblinking backdrop, like millions of eyes watching him. And behind him, Larry could *feel* rather than see the immense ponderous presence of the planet.

Campbell's voice crackled in his earphones. "Everybody ready?"

One by one, the eleven others answered by the numbers that had been hastily sprayed onto their suits.

"All right, everybody work to his left. Keep your guns loose."

Larry fingered the laser tool-turned-weapon at his waist. Sonic stunners wouldn't work in vacuum. If there was any shooting, somebody was going to die.

He began walking in a spiral around the big main wheel, his footsteps tacky in the magnetic boots. Around and around, spiraling like an electron in a strong magnetic field, curving from one connector tube to the next. There was practically no place for a man to hide here; the main level's outer wall was almost perfectly smooth, broken only by an occasional viewport.

Larry carefully avoided stepping on the viewports. Being plastiglass, they'd provide no grip for his magnetic boots. Larry didn't feel like slipping off the ship's surface. There were steering jets on his belt, but he preferred to stay in contact with the ship rather than try zooming through empty space.

At last he came to the next connector tube. He found that he was breathing hard, sweating, but feeling relieved. No sign of Dan. And that somehow made him almost happy.

At least I didn't have to shoot it out with him.

"Not yet," he heard himself mutter.

The others began reporting in. None of them had seen Dan.

"All right," Campbell said. "Every man goes along the tube he's at now. Stop at level two and report in."

It was taking too long, Larry realized. More than an hour had passed since they had first come outside. It would easily take another hour or more by the time they had checked out level two. It wasn't going to work. They'd have to go inside long before they could inspect level three. If Dan didn't show up soon, they'd have to call off the whole idea of searching outside for him. Unless they could get more people outside to help.

Larry always felt hot inside the suits. There was a radiator on the back of his lifepack, but it never seemed to get rid of his body heat fast enough. The air blowers whirred noisily, but he still found himself drenched with sweat before he was halfway up the tube to level two.

Around and around. Down was up, and then it was down again. He saw the planet swing by as he stolidly plodded along the metal skin of the tube. Stars and planet, turning, turning. *Keep your eyes searching for Dan!* he warned himself. But where? He could be crouched behind that antenna; Larry checked it out carefully. No. He could be hovering no more than a hundred meters from the ship, and he'd be virtually invisible

against the backdrop of stars. *We'd never see him . . .*
you'd have to be lucky enough to look in exactly the right
place at the right time . . .

And then Larry began to get the uncanny feeling that
Dan was walking along behind him, following his footsteps, tiptoeing the way children sometimes do behind
someone they're trying to surprise.

He knew it was silly, irrational. But the feeling grew.
He felt a cold shudder go through him. *If he is behind*
me . . .

Larry whirled around. It was a clumsy move in the
pressure suit, and his boots left contact with the ship. *No*
one! Then he realized he was drifting away. He slapped
at the control unit on his belt, and the microjets puffed
briefly and slammed him hard back onto the tube. His
knees buckled momentarily, but he stayed erect.

You're getting spooked, he raged at himself.

He glanced at the oxygen gauge on his wrist. Still in
the green, but a sliver of yellow was showing. When the
yellow went to red, he'd have to either go inside or get a
fresh tank.

His earphones buzzed. "Mr. Chairman?"

"Here."

"Just a moment, sir . . ."

Then Valery's voice said, "Larry? I think Dr. Hsai
might have come up with something."

"What?"

"Wait . . . I'll put him on."

Larry kept plodding on, kept his eyes searching.

"Mr. Chairman," the psychotech said formally.

"Doctor," Larry responded automatically.

"I've been reviewing my records of Dan Christopher's case."

"And?"

"I believe I may have found something significant."

Larry fumed inside his helmet. "Well, what is it?"

But there was no hurrying Hsai. "Do you recall when Mr. Christopher was first placed under my care . . . just after his father died?"

"Yes. Go on."

"He was treated for a few days and then released. I tried to maintain contact with him, to follow up his case."

"I know. We put him under observation for a month." *And you found nothing*, Larry added mentally.

"Yes. Exactly so. But before then—just after he was released from the infirmary for the first time, I asked him several times to check in with me for follow-up tests. He refused."

"So?"

Dr. Hsai's voice continued smoothly, with just the barest hint of excitement. "At one point, he warned me that his job was too important to be interfered with."

"Warned you?"

"I have his exact words here . . . listen . . ."

Larry stopped moving and hung frozen on the skin of the tube. The ship's vast turning motion swung him majestically around, like a lone rider on an ancient merry-go-round. Then he heard Dan's voice, which startled him for a moment, until he realized it was one of Dr. Hsai's tapes:

"Our reactors are feeding the ship's main rocket engines," Dan was saying hotly, "on a very, *very* carefully programmed schedule. This ship can't take more than a tiny thrust loading—we're simply not built to stand high thrust, it'd tear us apart . . ."

"Everyone knows this." Hsai's voice.

Dan answered, "Uh-huh. This is a very delicate part of the mission. A slight miscalculation or a tiny flaw in the reactors could destroy this ship and kill everyone."

Click.

"Do you understand what he was trying to tell me?" Dr. Hsai asked.

Larry blinked puzzledly. "Frankly, no. What he was saying was perfectly true."

"Of course. But underneath the obvious truth, he was threatening to destroy the ship and everyone in it if he didn't get his way."

"What?"

"I believe that is what is in his mind," Hsai went on. "Of course, I am no psychiatrist, but I think such an action of self-destruction would be consistent with Christopher's behavior pattern."

Larry instantly blurted, "The reactors!"

Val's voice came on. "Larry, do you think he'd do it?"

"We can't run the risk of *not* thinking it. Val, get the power crew on the phone and have them abandon level seven. Everybody out except a skeleton crew, and I want them in pressure suits. Quick!"

"Right."

Larry fumbled with the radio switches on his belt. "Mort, this is Larry." *Do I have the right frequency?*

"You find something?"

"No. I just got a call from inside. Hsai thinks Dan might try to blow the reactors."

"Holy . . ."

"I'm jetting up there. You keep the search going, just to make sure I'm not on a wild-goose chase."

"Okay."

Larry pushed off the tube wall and touched the micro-jet controls. He felt tiny hands grab him around the waist and push him up toward the ship's hub. The rings of the ship passed beneath him: three, four, five, six.

There was a flash and a puff of what looked like steam, up ahead at level seven. Something cartwheeled up, a jagged shard of metal. Larry steered in that direction.

Level seven's only viewport had been blown apart. The lights inside were gone. Larry grabbed the jagged rim of the exploded port and hauled himself in through the hole.

If I turn on my helmet lamp I'll be a certain target.

Something heavy and metallic slammed thunderously in the distance and a gust of wind tore past Larry, cracking like a miniature thunderclap.

Safety hatch! He's opened the safety hatch between the offices and the reactor area.

Larry reached to his belt with both hands, turned on his helmet lamp, and pulled the laser pistol from its holster.

The office was a shambles. When the viewport blew open, air pressure inside the office gusted violently out into space, bowling over everything in its path. Chairs were overturned, desk fittings broken and scattered over the floor. Any papers that had been around were blown outside.

But no bodies. Valery's warning must have reached the technicians just in time.

Larry hefted the pistol in his right hand and took a deep breath. The suit air suddenly tasted good. He moved toward the safety hatch that connected the office with the reactor area. In the low gravity of level seven, it was easy to move around, even inside the cumbersome suit. But still Larry moved slowly, cautiously. He was only moments behind Dan. Maybe he could surprise him.

The safety hatch was open, and the reactor area was deep in darkness. For a moment, Larry thought about switching off his helmet lamp. But he couldn't. *Be blind without it.*

He edged toward the hatch. It opened, he knew, onto a metal catwalk that hung above the two main working reactors and the main electrical power generator.

He stepped out onto the catwalk, then immediately flicked off his lamp.

Down below, kneeling by the power generator in a pool of light from his own helmet lamp, was Dan. He had a laser pistol in his hand, and he was burning it at full intensity on some of the exposed wiring of the generator. Smoke and sparks were sputtering from the generator's innards.

With barely a thought about what he was doing, Larry clambered over the catwalk's flimsy railing and launched himself at Dan. It was like a dream, a nightmare. He floated through the twenty meters separating them like a cloud drifting across the sky. Larry raised his right hand and threw his pistol as hard as he could at Dan. It banged into Dan's hand, knocking his own laser skittering across the floor. There was no sound.

Dan turned toward him, his lamp suddenly glaring

straight into Larry's eyes. Then they collided, hitting with a bone-jarring impact that carried the two of them up and over the generator and into a confused tangle of arms and legs onto the narrow floor space between the generator and one of the reactors.

It was like two robots grappling. In the low gravity, every strenuous move was overly done, and they fought clumsily, swinging, bouncing, rolling across the floor and flailing at each other. Noiselessly, except for the bone-carried shock of impact and the grunts that each man made inside his suit.

Larry's head was banged around inside his helmet a dozen times. His ears rang and he tasted blood in his mouth. Sweat was trickling stingingly into his eyes.

Dan was reaching up over Larry's shoulder, trying to grab his airline. Larry knocked his arm away and pushed Dan back against the smooth metal wall of the reactor. Dan bounced off, doubled over, and sliced Larry's legs, knocking him sprawling.

Feeling like a turtle on its back, Larry tried to scramble up again, but Dan was on top of him. Through the metal-to-metal contact of the suits, he could hear Dan faintly yelling something; it was unintelligible.

Dan had him by the shoulders now and was banging his head and torso against the metal floor plates. Each slam jarred Larry, blurred his vision. Either his suit was going to crack open or his head would; it didn't matter which one happened first.

He grappled his arms around Dan's torso, trying to hold on and prevent Dan from slamming him. But Dan just rode up and down on top of him, adding his own body's mass to the process of bludgeoning Larry to death. Larry's hands grasped frantically and closed on a slim piece of tubing. *Airline!* His first instinct was to rip it loose, but instead Larry simply squeezed on it, grabbed it hard and hung on.

In a few moments Dan stopped the pounding. He tried to reach Larry's arm, but Larry was wrapped too closely to him for that. Dan rolled over onto his back, but Larry hung on. Squeezing, squeezing the airline, keeping fresh oxygen from Dan's lungs, letting him suffocate on his own carbon dioxide.

Dan went limp.

Larry hung on for a few seconds longer, then let go. He himself sagged, barely conscious, on top of Dan's inert form. *No. Can't . . . pass out. He'll be coming around . . . as soon as fresh air . . . gets into his suit.*

Dazed, bloody, Larry got to his knees. He knew he couldn't stand up. He flicked on the helmet lamp and turned to look for the lasers. Dan's legs started to move feebly. Larry crawled on all fours, found one of the little pistols on the floor, and took it in his hand. He flopped into a sitting position, leaning his back against the generator, and pointed the pistol at Dan. With his free hand he worked the suit's radio switch.

"I've got him," he said weakly. "Reactor area."

Chapter 17

The Council members all looked happy enough, but Larry felt nothing but numbness inside himself.

Even Valery looked pleased. She had just shown all her data tapes about the Epsilon Indi planet. It looked as much like Earth, from this distance, as Earth itself did.

"I would like to suggest," Dr. Polanyi said, beaming across the table at her, "that Miss Loring be accepted as a member of the Council *pro tem*—for as long as her father is unable to attend our meetings."

There was a general nodding of heads and approving murmurs.

"Any dissenting voices?" Larry asked.

None.

"Then it's done."

There was only one empty seat at the table: Dan's. Larry glanced at it, his mouth tightening with bitterness.

Adrienne Kaufman cleared her throat. "What about the data we've just seen? Should we consider heading for this new planet? If not, we have a huge task of genetic work ahead of us."

Larry glanced around the table. None of the Council members seemed willing to speak before he did.

"Actually," he said at last, "I don't see any reason to

rush into such a decision. We're going to be here in orbit for many months, refurbishing the ship. Let's spend that time gathering more data about this new planet."

Valery said, "If we could build a bigger telescope, or improve the sensitivity of the instruments we have . . ."

"That could be done," Polanyi said quickly.

"Epsilon Indi is about the same distance from us as Alpha Centauri is from Earth," Larry said. "If we decide to go there, it will take another half-century."

"None of us will be awake for much of that trip," Polanyi said.

"If we decide to go," Adrienne Kaufman put in.

"Oh, I think we will," said the old engineer. "It looks too good to ignore."

The meeting broke up shortly after that. Valery got up from her chair and went toward Larry.

"They're putting Dan into cryosleep today. Dr. Tomaso says he can work on Dan's neural patterns much more easily when the nerve impulses are slowed down by the low temperature."

"I know," Larry said.

"He might be under cryosleep for years and years," she said.

He thought he knew what was bothering him, but he was afraid to mention it. Afraid she might tell him that his fears were correct.

She looked at him curiously. "I know what you're thinking."

"Do you?"

"Yes." Valery almost smiled. "You're wondering if I

want to go into cryosleep too, and be awakened when Dan's cured."

He reached out and took her hand. "Do you?"

"No," she said. "Silly. When are you going to believe that you're the one I want?"

He grinned foolishly. "Any day now."

They walked together out of the conference room and down a long, curving corridor. They stopped at a viewport and stared silently at the golden planet outside.

"It would've been a lovely world. . . ." Larry muttered. "So close . . . so close . . ."

"There's a better one waiting for us," Val said.

"But if we don't go into cryosleep," Larry realized, "we'll probably never see that new world."

She smiled up at him. "I know. But someone's got to keep the ship going, and raise a new generation of children who *will* see the new world. See it and live on it."

"Our children," he said.

"Human children," Val added. "Beautiful strong human men and women for the new world."

"For the new world," he echoed.

They smiled together and walked off down the corridor, arm in arm.